In the Realm of Demons

In the Realm of Demons

Imran Kureshi

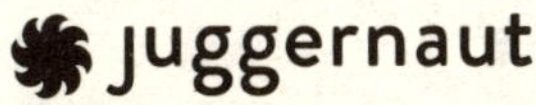

JUGGERNAUT BOOKS
KS House, 118 Shahpur Jat, New Delhi 110049, India

First published by Juggernaut Books 2019

10 9 8 7 6 5 4 3 2 1

P-ISBN: 978-93-5345-046-5
E-ISBN: 978-93-5345-047-2

Typeset in Adobe Caslon Pro by R. Ajith Kumar, Noida

Printed and bound at Thomson Press India Ltd

To Javed Masud

Contents

1

The Night of the Red Moon

Early memories of my cousin Koyel lingered in my mind like old flower petals pressed in the leaves of books, memories that were severed by unbelievable tragedy and subsequent greater events. I remember sitting with her in the jharokha of the palace as we played with her dolls. Don't get me wrong. I am a boy. But I enjoyed playing with her so much that I didn't care what the game was, and she would make it very interesting. I was twelve then and she a few months older. We were sort of kindred spirits, thrown together in that magnificent, venerable and haunted palace. Well, maybe it's not haunted in the regular sense; it is just that there is a curse on our family and what happened that dreadful and tragic night was indeed supernatural and undoubtedly my worst nightmare.

I better introduce myself. I'm Mehranullah Hashtpuri – Shahzada, mind you – son of Rani Sobia, the younger sister of Nawab Kaisar Khan of Hashtpur, and Koyel was the daughter of the nawab himself, from an earlier marriage. My father was not frugal with money and had died penniless in a hunting accident. The nawab had graciously taken in my mother and me so I could have the upbringing that befitted my lineage.

However, in the palace I found myself a second-class citizen, since the enfants de roi were Shehzad and Shehbaz, the sons of the nawab's principal wife, Shahzadi Lailat-u-Nisa, who belonged to the royal family of King Zahir Shah of Afghanistan. I was made acutely conscious that everything in the palace, the arras from France, the 'Goordner' (Gardner) crockery from Afghanistan, the beautiful porcelain figurines from Europe, the sensual statues from Italy, the Chinese vases and resplendent hand-cut glass from Russia, all belonged to the real heirs and I was only there on their sufferance. If Shehzad or Shehbaz told me to polish their shoes I would have to do it if I wanted to continue to enjoy my royal status. Often I felt rebellious, but my mother would quickly hush me. I could bear my own demeaned position, but when the members of the house put down or criticized my mother I couldn't stand it.

The rani was a haughty woman who believed that authority has to be asserted if it is to be retained. Maybe she had other intentions as well, but I was too young to understand these intrigues at the time. Not that she was wilfully nasty. Quite the opposite, instead. She was courtesy itself when talking to us personally, but her attitude and directives were tyrannical otherwise. Nobody was allowed to disagree with her opinions and sometimes her remarks were very barbed and hurtful. Her inaccessibility at crucial moments was insidious. Perhaps she did feel a bit threatened by the favour the nawab showed us. Under her administration even the servants assumed airs of self-importance and often controlled various facilities like the food that was served to us or the clothes that were to be stitched for us. I remember reading how Aurangzeb had served the head of Prince Dara Shikoh to Shahjahan on a platter. Well, comparing our situation to that may be an exaggeration, but I definitely felt it was only a difference of degree when often we would be served our meals and under the ornate dish cover would be only one kebab or a small smattering of saalan. The alternative in order to get a full meal from that royal larder was to eat in the main dining room with Her Majesty, where the food was always lavish, but that was another source of indigestion. Nobody could start before her and she always took her time to come. Even after she arrived, nobody could have as much as a glass of water till she had drunk some, or touch anything till she had helped herself. The slightest hint of bad behaviour by the children would lead to them being rebuked and sent off from the table before they could eat. I would often think about how people outside probably envied us living in this grand palace. Little did they know of the unhappiness within.

I also felt bad about the way Koyel was treated; sometimes I'd privately seethe with anger but would have to keep quiet. Nobody talked much about her mother. The shahzadi always spoke of Koyel as if she was the illegitimate daughter of a concubine, and this always hurt the poor little girl grievously. She was brought up by a faithful ayah and a spinster grand-aunt, Begum Qurat-ul-Ain, whom we called Badi Baaji. She was half mad. I equated Koyel's fate with my own, but her story is more dramatic and romantic than mine. I vaguely remember hearing about my mamoon, the present nawab, having a secret love marriage before his ascension. Koyel had been born in a hospital; we were all born in the palace. When the old nawab Mahmud Khan found out my mamoon had run away with his wife, he sent his guards after them. They were caught and brought back. Even then Kaisar Khan had refused to divorce his wife. It was said the old nawab had the nikahnama burnt and the entry in the Eidgah register deleted. As for the wife, an evil courtier suggested that they lock her for one night in the old pavilion outside the compound of the palace. It was supposed to be infested with snakes and people didn't even venture there in the day. However, in the morning the guards could not find her body. Apparently she somehow managed to escape during the night. The nawab sent people to search for her and bring her back but they could find neither hide nor hair of her. That was the last we heard of her. Maybe there was foul play. All great families have skeletons in the cupboard, especially kshatriya royalty.

Nawab Kaisar Khan seemed very fond of his daughter. He was also fond of my mother and me and always treated us kindly, making it a point to check that we were being given our due, but he was busy most of the time. He ruled the kingdom outside, but the proud rani ruled the household. The nawab thought it politic not to interfere in the domestic hierarchy.

As for my afternoons in the jharokha with Koyel, they were like luminous stained-glass images in the kaleidoscope of unsatisfactory, incomplete, sometimes happy, sometimes not, memories of my childhood – literally bathed in a dim, coloured radiance because the jharokha had coloured glass windows that muted the heat of the long and unending summer afternoons. I found a sort of magic in the company of my gentle cousin. She had commandeered this place as her private nook. It had a balcony that overlooked the elephants' courtyard, not that we had elephants any longer. Now we kept only one that was used to be weighed against a mountain of metal coins on the nawab's birthday, which were then distributed among the poor. In the olden days it used to be bricks of silver.

There the two of us would sit together. She had a large collection of dolls and we would select some to make a doll family – a mother doll, a father doll and several smaller ones designated as children. Koyel had another set of puppet dolls, the kind that hanjan* puppeteers make. They were all Mughal royalty, and of these one was her favourite – a female doll that was supposed to be Anarkali. Using chairs, boxes, a veil and bed sheets, Koyel would build a charming abode that not only housed the dolls but had enough space for us to sit and have tea with the doll family. Then she would take out her pièce de résistance, a miniature tea set, complete with shiny cutlery and fancy cups. Sitting with her in the facsimile of domestic bliss she had built, I was able to identify her natural body odour. It was a light, musty smell, like that of groundnuts. Though not of any perfume, I found it exceedingly appealing, as it sort of embodied her very essence – her delicate, smooth-skinned presence. As the afternoon would draw on, I would take secret sniffs of her, trying to take in as much of her scent as possible. She also had incredibly shapely hands and feet, and eyes that I could get lost in. Nobody can imagine how enchanting I found it just to be with her. When I look

---

* Gypsy

back on that time, it seems those afternoons never ended.

It must have been August 1945 when the trouble started. The daughter of a scythe was said to have become possessed by a demon. Her cries, shrieks and violent fits were disturbing the peace of the lower servants' quarters. They could be heard even in the upper storeys of the palace, which is when the rani decided to settle the matter. She had the girl summoned to the palace to show her to a doctor. He was the MS in charge of the charitable hospital of the state. The shahzadi considered this talk of possession to be superstitious nonsense and wanted to prove her benevolence to the servants by curing the girl in a proper medical manner. She was brought into the main hall of the palace and all of us – womenfolk and children – huddled behind the curtains of the pillars to witness the macabre presence. I remember her face well. She was only a young girl, hardly twelve. She was frail, unkempt, had sharp features heightened by undernourishment and wild eyes that I found frightening. Of course, she was innocuous and insane, but to us her behaviour seemed a treasonous disregard for the regal rani. A rational person would be moved to pity at the sight, but I was terrified to see her, knowing that this person could do terrible things to herself and maybe others. Pity made the situation seem more of a travesty. I would rather face a raging tiger than confront her in her passion.

The rani showed great magnanimity, ignoring the

snarls, terrifying sounds and lewd gestures the girl made. However, when the doctor tried to examine her, she struggled so much that her parents could hardly hold her down. She let out a deep, ululating, petrified cry and the next moment she was in the air, as if somebody had flung her upwards, and when she landed on the ground, her head hit the hard marble floor with a resounding crack. I was sure she must have fractured her skull. As she lay there spasmodically jerking her limbs, frothing at the mouth, rolling her eyes and uttering animal sounds, I remember thinking that the demon must have thrown her upwards and these must be her dying convulsions from having broken her head. The doctor quickly gave her an injection and she calmed down. The rani looked pleased, as if this meant that the girl had been cured. The doctor examined her, wrote down several medicines for her and the servants carried the poor girl out on a charpai.

After that evening I was always careful to avoid the part of the hall where she had fallen. The way she had burbled just before she was thrown up seemed to indicate she had seen something ghastly, and I was scared it might still be lurking somewhere there, invisible. Later we learnt that the medicines had no effect on the girl and the parents had to send for a local amil to perform an exorcism.

That was the night it happened, and I am convinced the source of the dreadful occurrence was the demon released by the so-called exorcism. It had been a very hot and stuffy day and sunset didn't seem to settle the dust of the afternoon, in fact there was a thunderstorm brewing on the horizon with distant flickers of lightning. The rani had forbidden us to go to the servants' quarters, but one servant companion of mine, Amin, my tutor's son, took me there, thrilled by the event.

It was very smelly with the buffalos tied nearby and all the servants milling around in the hot night. The place was lit by lanterns, since the compound of the quarters was unlit, and a big fire was burning. Amin explained to me that it was a demon of fire and the flames would coax it out. An assistant of the amil was beating a drum. The girl was standing unbound in front of the exorcist. I must say he had greater control over her than the doctor had had, because though she growled, spat, snarled and made dreadful faces at him, sometimes lunging at him with clawed hands, when he would command her to stop she would hold back, showing him utter hate but desisting from attacking him. Sometimes she would start to slink backwards, away from the amil, but again when he would tell her to stop she would halt. Once in retaliation to his command she ran towards him with a hideous expression on her face and I was certain that this time she would attack him, but the amil stood his ground and ordered her to stop. She squirmed and twisted threateningly but didn't attack him, behaving like some vicious animal bent on causing mayhem but fettered by some invisible leash. Perhaps the amil would prove more efficacious than the doctor. There certainly seemed to be some inexplicable rapport between them. It couldn't have been a tacit understanding, because then the amil began to burn chillies around the girl and even though we were watching from a distance our eyes started smarting. He was blowing the chillies right into the girl's face to make it so uncomfortable for the demon that it would be forced to leave the girl. She let out unearthly bellowing howls that surely her young female vocal chords could not have been capable of producing, and her hate seemed to increase.

However, if I had in any way felt that this amil was going to cure the girl, when I looked at his face I suddenly felt differently. There was no kindness in his eyes. He had deep furrows down his cheeks, such that it was difficult to tell his age, or even determine if he was young or old; his pointy beard was hennaed a violent red and his eyes, dark and intense, seemed to mask sinister knowledge. I got a wave of adverse vibes; he looked completely evil. Some people looked on very seriously. I heard that after communing with the demon (I missed that part), the amil had warned everybody that when the entity left the girl, before it was banished, it could descend on anyone around. So we were not without danger. When the amil began threatening the girl with a live snake I could stand it no longer. I told Amin I was leaving and went back to the palace.

There I found everybody on the balcony overlooking

the quarters, watching the exorcism with curiosity. However, the activity had made our spinster grand-aunt, the half-mad one, more perturbed than usual.

'Child, do not believe them. They are not what they seem. There is something very wrong,' she said conspiratorially to me. 'I'll tell my nephew when he returns; he always listens to me.'

'Who are not what they seem, Badi Baaji?' I asked.

But she didn't answer my question because the next moment she gasped. 'Look at the moon! It's red!'

We looked up at the hazy sky and saw the moon was indeed red. It did not just have a chromatic red outline – its luminous surface was not silvery, but a swirling, dusky red.

With the macabre goings-on below, this terrified us more than anything else. Of course, in retrospect I realized that this was probably some refractive phenomenon caused by the red dust of the ground in the air. At the time, however, my grand-aunt became almost hysterical. 'The curse! The curse! Call the rani! Get the taweez and send Shehbaz away from here! Save him! Save him!'

My mother also became worried. Everybody was ushered inside from the balcony. The rani came in frantically and rushed Shehzad and Shehbaz to her room, ordering a servant to call the chauffeur to get the car out. My instinctive reaction was to look at Koyel, but her ayah and the grand-aunt were protectively leading her away as well.

My mother looked at me. She too was scared and said, 'Come, son. We'll also lock ourselves up in our room.'

'Wait, Mother, I think the nawab is coming back,' I told her, because through the trees I could see some car lights coming up the long driveway.

This reassured her somewhat. She stepped back on to the balcony to take a look.

'What is the curse, Mother?' I asked.

'I'll recite it for you,' she said.

When the moon is red,
Sana hath said,
What thou doth dread,
Shall rise from the dead,
And Hashtpur's heir behead.

'Who is Sana, Mother?'

'Don't you know? He was your ancestor from Chandullah's side of the family, your relatives who live in the old quarters. He used to be the nawab ages ago. Ranjit Singh defeated him in 1845. He placed Sanaullah's brother Farhatullah on the throne of Hashtpur. Our side of the family stems from Nawab Farhatullah and we have ruled Hashtpur since then. Sanaullah was beheaded. On the day of his execution, Sanaullah pronounced this curse on his brother's family. Nawab Farhatullah died a short while after under mysterious circumstances. He was found with a broken neck and they say when they tried to lift him his head flopped downwards. Following this incident, on a night when the moon was red, his son Sabqatullah disappeared. His younger brother Raghbatullah became the ruler. It seems the curse falls only on the firstborn. The British beheaded Raghbatullah's son Syedullah. They say the moon was red on that night too. However, your great-great-grandfather Faizullah ruled for many years. He died fighting the Ghakkars and since he had no heir his cousin Janullah was made the nawab. When the first full moon was red, he was found with his head ripped off in the old pavilion. Thereafter, it is said, Janullah's son got a powerful taweez made by a powerful pir, which has since protected the family from the curse. It is handed down from generation to generation. In the past three generations, only one eldest son was found decapitated, so we had hoped the curse had been lifted.'

'So you and I are safe, Mother,' I said relieved.

'I suppose so. We are not the heirs. But there are tales of other deaths too. Let's pray Shehbaz is safe. Come, we better lock ourselves in our room till the nawab comes,' she said anxiously.

My mother says I have a strong sense of smell. Suddenly I sniffed a strange and beautiful scent. Most perfumes have familiar smells, of roses, lavender, oodh and such. But this perfume was completely alien; I couldn't identify it with anything. It caused a nice sensation inside me with a fragrant twist.

'By the way, that's a beautiful perfume you're wearing, Mother,' I said.

'No, that's not my perfume. I smell it too,' she answered.

The next moment there was a loud wail from the quarters below and at once all the lights and lanterns went off. The lights of the palace also flickered, before everything plunged into darkness. I thought I saw a deeper blackness swirl up from below and then the quarters were filled with shrieks and screams.

'What's happened? What's happened?' my mother cried, clasping me tightly.

'I don't know! Maybe the demon is loose,' I answered. Huddled together, we rushed through the dark doorway of the balcony. The full moon and dusty haze outside gave the sky a luminescence and we could make our way through the familiar rooms with the help of the slight light coming in from the windows.

'Where is everybody?'

'Let's go towards the main hall,' I suggested. Nawab sahib must have arrived by now.'

Holding each other's hand tightly, we crept through the darkened rooms, panic rising inside us. We wondered what was happening. Why were the servants screaming?

Why had the electricity gone off? Was there some real danger?

As we passed the long side gallery adjacent to the main balustrade, I saw the curtains at the end leap up with a glow and catch fire. I couldn't believe this was happening. The curtains were definitely blazing. This was no hallucination, and then in the light, I saw a monstrous form. It seemed humanoid with the legs of a goat, but its shape appeared to twist and change as it came leaping towards us.

'Run, Mother!' I shouted, not paying attention to any obstacles on the way as I pulled her along by her hand. Thank goodness she didn't trip while I half dragged, half carried her with me.

Desperately we reached the alcove above the balustrade. The lights from below made it easier for us to see. The nawab and several of his men were in the hall holding lanterns and torches. The creature seemed to have disappeared, maybe due to the light, but there was still a glow where the curtains had been burning. We rushed down the stairs.

'Sobia bhan! Where are the others?' the nawab shouted anxiously.

'Kaisar bhai! Kaisar bhai! Thank heavens you've come. There is something awful behind us!'

At once two men with spears and guns started to rush up the stairs, but the venerable Zamurrad Shah told them not to go, because there was nothing they could do about what was up there. Zamurrad Shah was the nawab's astrologer and spiritual adviser.

'Everybody is hiding in their rooms,' Sobia told the nawab, looking anxiously at the alcove above the main hall.

The nawab had the dinner gong sounded to summon everybody, but it wasn't necessary because hearing that he had arrived all the members of the royal family began to emerge from their rooms and enter the hall, carrying candles and fancy lanterns. The diwan came out of the nawab's study. 'Here is the taweez, Your Highness,' he said, handing him a large gold necklace.

'The curse! The curse!' the shahzadi uttered anxiously. 'The moon was red. Save your heir Shehbaz, Nawab sahib!'

'Shehbaz sahib, Shehbaz sahib, come forward,' a servant said officiously.

'Yes, I saw the moon too,' the nawab said. 'That's why I rushed back. Everybody, stand near the taweez. Where is Koyel?' he asked, looking around and holding the taweez high in the air.

'Mehran beta, come close to us,' he said to me, since I was standing a little away.

I was still looking up at the alcove, hoping the creature wouldn't attack us with all these people and lights. I thought I saw a shadow move behind an arch.

'Sir, there is something up there,' I told the nawab.

'Yes! Yes! I know. There's nothing we can do about that right now. Come here, you'll be safer,' he said earnestly. Concerned, he looked around again and repeated, 'Where is Koyel? Somebody get Koyel!'

Now I began to worry about Koyel. She and Badi Baaji were the only people who weren't here yet. The diwan quickly set off towards the passage leading to the grand-aunt's suite on the ground floor, his gas lantern casting monstrous shadows.

'Nawab sahib! Nawab sahib! Here is Shehbaz!' the shahzadi said anxiously, coming up to him. 'Put the taweez on him.'

'Shahzadi, he is not my heir! He is in less danger!' the nawab practically exploded. 'My heir is my eldest child, Koyel. Get her quickly!'

At this moment, we saw three forms coming through the passage – the diwan ushering the smaller figure of Koyel and the grand-aunt hurrying behind them as fast as she could.

'Here I am, Daddy,' she said and came running forward.

'Quick! Come and put on the taweez,' the nawab said, bending down and opening his arms to hold her.

I thought somebody had opened a vial of perfume because suddenly I smelt a strong whiff of an enrapturing scent, like a breath of fresh, fragrant air, reminiscent of stars and the stratosphere. For a second I was relieved that Koyel was safe. But the next moment a palpable darkness swept through the hall, engulfing all of us, and as the nawab clasped the young girl to his bosom, he found he was only holding her Anarkali doll. I heard a sigh disappear into an unfathomable distance, and then the lights came on again.

2

The End of an Era

It really seemed as if the tragedy changed everything. My childish mind just couldn't comprehend that my cousin had been slain, especially because of the circumstances – one moment she was there, the next she was gone! I couldn't believe she was dead. Her absence left me feeling grievously desolate. I dearly wished she would just turn up one day as if nothing had happened and we could be together again. But she never did and deep within I knew she wouldn't. With the passage of time I managed to put her out of my head, but I was never able to put her out of my heart.

The nawab was deeply affected. There was more to her death than merely the tragedy. After that night the family sort of broke up. The unity of the household had always been tenuous anyhow. Even as a child I could tell that there had always been some kind of intrigue going on, though I did not know what it was about. I suppose at that time I was too young to understand. However, it suddenly became apparent that we couldn't go on living together. It seemed as if some of our relatives and state officials started showing enmity towards others. This antagonism was clearly directed towards us and I was surprised by the radical change in the behaviour of some of them towards my mother and me and even poor Badi Baaji. My uncle tacitly gave my mother our mansion in Lahore and we, with Badi Baaji, left the old, historical palace where I had passed my early childhood. But the pomp and luxury of the place had mainly focused on the shahzadi's side of the family and only the lees had fallen to our lot, so I for one was not sorry to go. There were no nice associations left of the place for me. I had no reason to live there any more.

In retrospect I can be more philosophical about my sojourn there as a 'prince' of the realm. I suppose every grand and beautiful monument in history has some tragedy, some deep feelings of sorrow suffered by the artisans, builders or others connected with it embedded in its walls. Even my mother was happy to migrate to Zeenat Mahal. At last she could lead the life she wanted and raise me in the proper manner, without anyone making me feel subordinate to them – as if *I* could ever feel inferior, heh, heh! – and to give me the sort of life she felt I should have. The nawab had bestowed a handsome allowance on her and for one year Shahzadi Sobia enjoyed an opulent lifestyle in Lahore. We had a grand holiday in Simla. She threw lavish parties and held mushairas and concerts, inviting the most famous musicians from all over India. We became quite the centre of society. British officials, poets and prominent Congress and Muslim League politicians attended our functions; even such Britishers who regarded the 'natives' with scorn were keen to dance attendance at Zeenat Mahal. Since Koyel's tragic death involved the family curse, nobody ever spoke of it and we kept the circumstances secret. I started going to school, instead of having private tutors, which was much better. Though I was very mediocre in studies, I found I was good at horse riding because of my early training in the state. I had also been taught fencing in the estate but there was no institution for it in Lahore. However, riding was a special feature in our school and later I made it into the tent-pegging team that participated in the National Horse and Cattle Show.

Another of my interests was music. My mother had always wanted me to pursue it. Since famous musicians were coming to our house, she used the opportunity to hire a music teacher for me. After trying various instruments I started learning the bansuri. I became quite good at it and would often sit in the garden and play. I didn't miss Qila Rajwaran at all. I was happy and so was my mother.

Perhaps the tragedy had grieved the nawab much more than I imagined, because he passed away before the year was out. Shehbaz became the nawab. Since he was only twelve, the rani ran the kingdom. She stopped my mother's allowance and filed a case against us for Zeenat Mahal. Then I found out the astronomical costs of my mother's grand functions. I wished she had saved some of her money and I realized that though she could be a gracious and impeccable hostess, she was hopeless at taking care of herself or managing her finances. I was only thirteen but the responsibility of looking after the two ladies fell on my shoulders. I also had to follow up the case in court. Afsar, our faithful old chauffeur from Hashtpur, was very helpful. However, every day I was very scared that the shahzadi would send a jeep-load of soldiers from the state's army and evict us, but fortunately the Partition, with its gory aftermath, solved this problem. It spelt the end of the era of princely states.

This was a period of upheaval and insurmountable difficulties for us, the biggest one being finding a source of income. The new country was formed with a lot of patriotic fervour, in a spirit of cooperation, with assertions of religion and nationalism and political activity among the general public on the one hand and government officials getting down to settling matters as well as assuming power and facilities on the other (even deputy commissioners had flags on their cars) while rich landlords enjoyed lavish lifestyles. There was a great transformation. Almost all the old Hindu shops, flour mills and workshops closed down, but were soon reopened, albeit inefficiently, under local ownership. Of course, these were primarily teething problems; but in many cases, as for the country as a whole, they were not. The previous plural society with its presence of Hindus and Sikhs and their practices ceased to exist altogether, though many Britishers continued to hold positions of control in society as they had been doing in the past. There was a constant threat of an attack by India and there was also rampant inflation. Sadly, the founder of the nation died shortly afterwards.

Somehow we survived this period. We kept cutting down on expenses and selling jewellery and other possessions to meet our day-to-day needs. Then Afsar Khan suggested we sell part of the land of our house that faced the main road. Of course, my spirit rebelled against this prospect, but we had to do something. Fortunately, in this transaction the unbelievable inflation proved to be a boon. I found out commercial land had become very expensive and I had to sell a surprisingly small strip to get enough capital for a moderately regular income. I requisitioned a bit more land there and built a few shops of our own. Unfortunately, we had to forgo our double driveway for a single one. However, it was a huge lawn and even after selling the land it was big enough to play a cricket match in (I suppose originally you could play polo on it). My mother was extremely impressed by how

I had handled the situation. Baaji wasn't quite aware of what was happening and when I started constructing a wall at the far end of the lawn she became frantic and wanted to call the guards to stop the intruders from building on our land. I felt my uncle's spirit turning in his grave at what I had done.

As for Nawab Shehzad, his reign only lasted a little over a year. Hashtpur acceded to India after Partition and with the beginning of political integration in India it became what was termed a salute state of a princely union and Shehzad a member of the presidium, which meant you watch someone else rule your kingdom and the government eat your revenue. As compensation the government paid him an allowance from the privy purse, which meant he became the government's paid employee. No doubt the allowance was substantial, but it was an 'allowance'. Well, that's the way the cookie crumbles. At least our income (my mother's and mine) was our own and we weren't subservient to anyone. I also heard that the state had run up huge debts and the government had taken over Rajwarana. Imagine, for centuries the fort had repelled invading armies and now a banker armed with a briefcase had come and taken over it.

Thus, the years passed. I preferred this life. With hindsight my earlier days in the palace didn't seem too bad, especially because of my time with Koyel, like a dream dreamt long ago that couldn't affect me now.

During our stay in Hashtpur, Ijazuddin chacha, an old revenue government officer posted in the palace by the British, had developed a feeling of fealty for our family. He now lived in Lahore and would drop in every Eid and on other occasions to pay his respects to my mother. He would always bring a cake and give us news of the state.

~

The year 1956 rolled around. I'd given my HSC and the winter vacations had started. Along with tent-pegging I was part of the polo team in school and later began to play in the polo club as a member of the team of the 5th Lancers.

It is important to mention two small incidents involving my flute playing during this period. I said I was good, but the truth is I was erratic, like I am in everything I do. Once I was playing the flute for some of my mother's guests and I got so lost in the melody that I enthralled my audience. Mrs Sirosh, a friend of my mother's, commented that the bansuri was such a sad instrument. One of the guests was a famous poet and he remarked that only someone with deep sadness in his heart could play like that. I was glad none of my tent-pegging chums were around to hear this comment.

Another time I was playing the flute on the roof at night. Again I got carried away with the music and I felt that I had never played so beautifully before. What a pity I didn't have an audience. I continued playing, surpassing myself, sending the melodious notes up to the stars in the dark, lonely night. The strange part was that even when I wanted to conclude I was loath to do so and it was a good half-hour before I could bring myself to stop.

Sometimes I wondered if Zeenat Mahal was haunted.

~

It was a grand palace with huge pillars, tall French windows and towering cornices, but with its thick walls and deep verandas there were surprisingly few rooms. The upper portion was given to my grand-aunt and sometimes she wouldn't come down for days. On other nights we'd sit together after dinner and my mother would make paan for us from her huge, ornate paandaan that always lay on the takht on which she sat, as we talked of this, that and the other. Sometimes at night I would creep into my mother's bedroom to cuddle and sleep with her, though I was a teenager. She liked this too and it made us feel secure. I was very fond of her Je Reviens perfume. It had an after-smell that reminded me of the palace ladies' rich robes, still retaining the remnants of expensive attars. I felt sorry for Baaji, living alone upstairs with no such beautiful haven to turn to.

Baaji had dreams and sometimes when we sat together she would tell us about them.

'Last night I saw Kaisar bhai. He was wearing a beautiful gold-thread robe with a paisley line down the front and an orange turban. However, he seemed very disturbed. I kept trying to draw his attention as he walked by with his retinue but he was so distracted he didn't notice me.

Then one day Badi Baaji told us about a dream she had had about Zamurrad Shah (he too had passed away a few years ago).

'He was sitting alone in the munshikhana and kept looking sideways as if he was scared of something. He showed me a shard of coloured glass and told me this was all that was left. He told me to give the old taweez to Nawabzada Mehran. But when he turned to the safe behind him there was nothing there. He got extremely upset and then he handed me the ruby my nephew used to wear on his royal turban. He told me to give that to Mehran.'

'If he were here he would have been able to tell us what this means,' my mother commented. 'It's not good to have dreams about receiving presents from people who have died.'

'Well, I didn't receive any ruby,' I remarked somewhat facetiously.

'Yes, but Baaji took it in her dream. In fact, it's not good to talk to dead people in dreams either.'

'No, no. He was trying to tell me something, something important,' the old lady asserted. 'The shard of glass was a sign that the palace, the old kingdom had fallen to ruin.'

'Yes, I heard about that. The palace was taken over by the government, but fell into disuse and has been occupied by gypsies,' I told them.

'See, my dreams are never wrong. The details are important. The fact that Zamurrad sends a ruby for Mehran beta is very significant. The ruby has the power to protect warriors. All Rajputs wore rubies when they went to battle. Zamurrad was sending a warning to you, beta. You better get a ruby ring and be very careful,' Begum Qurat-ul-Ain said, taking out a small quantity of opium from a silk bag and putting it into her paan.

'Who's he warning me against, my maths teacher?' I quipped.

'Oh dear,' said my mother, worried. 'Beta, you better take my old ruby ring from the locker and wear it.'

'Ammi jaan, you sold that. Don't you remember?'

'Oh dear, can't we buy another?'

'Please don't believe in these superstitions.'

~

However, my stoic scepticism about superstitions suffered a complete reversal that very night. I was sound asleep in my room when I had a strange dream. You know how sometimes you have a dream about yourself sleeping and it feels like you are awake, well, it must have been one of those. Or maybe it was a hallucination or something; it was so intense, or perhaps I *was* awake and it was real. In the middle of the night I felt someone wake me. I don't know whether someone shook me or called me, but the next moment it seemed I was sitting up. In the dim light of the room I saw a figure at the end of the bed – a young female figure. I tried to focus. The figure whispered earnestly, 'Meeru! Meeru bhai, wake up! Wake up! Listen to me.'

Even in my confused state something in her voice gripped my heart.

'Listen to me,' she repeated. 'Your life is in danger.'

It took me a few seconds to gather my senses. The figure anxiously came closer to the head of my bed and leaned forward. She was now quite close to me.

'I can't stay but I must warn you against the curse,' the figure hissed.

She was about my age and suddenly in the half-light I saw that her eyes were those of Koyel, and then I noticed her face – different, no longer that of a little girl, but unmistakably hers. If that wasn't enough I got a whiff from her person as she bent over me and I recognized her odour, except it was more feminine and mature.

'Koyel, is that you?' I mumbled and tried to touch her.

But the next moment she was gone and I found myself lying on the bed in semi-darkness.

I felt as if I had been hit by a bombshell. Yes, that could be no one else but Koyel, though not the little girl I remembered. She was as she would have been today had she not died. It was definitely her smell. Was she reaching out to me from beyond the grave, trying to warn me about something? But dead people don't grow up, or do they? Dead people don't have their characteristic body smells; their breath doesn't waft upon one. Had my imagination constructed all this?

No, I told myself. The warning must be serious for Koyel to have come from the dead or wherever she was. I was certain I had seen Koyel in the flesh – what she would look like grown up, what she would smell and sound like, the expression in her eyes. Was it at all possible that somehow, somewhere, Koyel was alive?

I ran to my mother's room and woke her up. I excitedly yammered about what I had seen. It took quite a few minutes for her to understand what I was suggesting.

'It was only a dream, dear,' she said, patting my cheek. 'Your mind must be worked up. Though we don't talk of Koyel, her memory has not left our hearts in all these years.'

Like old flower petals in the pages of books, a thought from a poem occurred to me.

'But, Ammi, believe me, I really saw her. At first I couldn't recognize her. She'd grown over the years.

If it was just my mind, I would have seen her how I remember her – as a little girl!'

'Your imagination can play wondrous tricks. Go to sleep. We'll talk about it in the morning. But heed the warning. Badi Baaji also had a dream warning you of danger.'

3

The Quest for a Dream

At twelve o'clock, reveille time in Zeenat Mahal, my mother and I discussed my dream over breakfast.

'Beta, you must be very careful. Your vision was similar to Badi Baaji's dream about some impending danger. Shahji used to say powerful demons have such a strong spiritual presence that their actions and proximity can affect our dreams. I remember before the dreadful night poor Koyel was snatched by the demon, Badi Baaji had a dream about one of Koyel's dolls giving her a ruby.'

'Ammi, believe me, Koyel is not dead. Somehow, somewhere, she is alive. My dream proved that,' I said emotionally.

'Please, Meeru, don't get your hopes up. It's impossible. No one can survive a curse, unless you have a taweez like Bhaijaan had. She's been gone for ten years. If, as you believe, she is alive, surely in this time we would have got some news of her; she would have tried to contact us. Life has its tragedies and we have to accept them. After all these years, don't open past wounds, beta. Let the past be in our memories. But heed the warning in your dream.'

'Yeah. Sure. But who would want to harm me? She said something about warning me against the curse. Well, all that is left behind in India. The state is practically non-existent and we've got nothing to do with it in any case. What was she trying to warn me about?'

'Yes, it doesn't make sense. But clearly we have been warned and I fear the threat is supernatural. We have seen demons and know what they can do. I'm very worried. Can't we buy a ruby? Will that be good enough? I wish Badi Baaji could tell us more. This not knowing is dreadful. I've heard there's a famous amil in Ichhra. Maybe you should go see him,' she said, distraught.

To me the danger didn't seem real or urgent. I was only keen to find out whether I had seen Koyel alive. I went to my mentor and guide and told him all about it.

'Afsar Khan, this is what I dreamt or actually saw last night. I know she's alive. How can I find her? I have to find her!'

'It does seem strange. I think the only thing to do is to consult someone who knows about demons and such things. But you better be careful. There is clearly some danger.'

'But who would want to harm me?'

'Who knows, we don't understand these things. I advise you to always carry a pistol. I'll get you a small two-two gun with four bullets. It's flat and fits in the pocket without being visible.'

'What good is a pistol against demons?'

'We don't know what the danger is. Keep the pistol with you at all times just in case.'

Afsar had also heard of the amil in Ichhra, so we decided to consult him.

We bought the pistol and went to see the seer. I must say he had a full-fledged clinic. We had to sit in the waiting room with other 'patients' – you've got to be sick to see such a guy. He had a consulting room and often checked his patients with a stethoscope and took their blood pressure because most of them came complaining of some ailment that they believed had been induced by magic or needed magic to be cured. He had an 'operating theatre' which had a dark alcove made of black rocks with niches in it containing lighted diyas and a sort of pagan altar in front of it festooned with garlands. His patients had to kneel in front of it and he would wave magic circles around their heads. Anyway, I found his prognosis to be too much like something out of Amir Hamza. I had seen demons and knew they were not like what he described.

We left quickly. I asked Afsar, 'Any other ideas?'

On the way we stopped at a crossing and a eunuch

came towards us clapping her hands and asking us for alms. There was a group of them operating at this spot. This gave me another idea. The eunuchs here had a closely knit widespread community and lived in the old city. I got out of the car and gave her more money than she would have expected. I told her I needed some urgent advice and wanted to meet the best ustad of magic in the city. I explained that my life was in danger and I needed to see a seer who had genuine knowledge about magic and demons, promising her more money if she helped me. She believed me. These people have their own hexes and tonas. I saw sympathy in her eyes and felt she would have obliged even if I hadn't paid her. She made a sincere effort and consulted with her companions. One of them volunteered to take us to someone called Hakeem Zafar Basra. She got in the car and we drove to the old city. We walked through narrow lanes overhung by balconies and arrived at a three-storey building, ensconced between two other tenements, that was clearly very, very old. It had very fine plasterwork that nobody could do these days and the balcony had a fairly intricate wooden trellis. The facade, though whole and uncracked, teetered a bit to one side. Perhaps it was the structures, all packed close together, that held each other up.

The hakeem had his shop on the first floor. He seemed incredibly old, with a long, silky white beard. Age seemed to have thinned his fingers and limbs and made them more graceful. He sat us down courteously and offered us tea, which was welcome on this cold day. I described to him my dream about Koyel and told him that I felt she was alive. He looked serious and told us that only a very powerful pir could provide protection against a jinn that had already been summoned. He didn't know of anyone who did that any more. In the olden days sorcerers used black magic and bandish karras* to summon demons and do their bidding. However, that was a forgotten art. He added, 'Even if someone knew the rituals, who in this day and age would dare invoke such demons unless there was someone to guide them.' However, he gave me a taweez that could offer some protection.

Then he told us all about jinns. He said they existed in a parallel world that sometimes overlapped ours. He explained that humans were made of mud, whereas jinns were of two types, either of fire or of air. He informed us that contrary to popular belief, they smelt fragrant† because they were made of air and fire. Since mud is more solid than these elements, it was possible for jinns to enter this world but not for humans to enter theirs, though in ancient times there were sorcerers who crossed this barrier. Though it was forbidden for jinns to make this transition, they are capricious, evil creatures and

---

*Pentacles

† *Lemegeton* or *The Lesser Key of Solomon* mentions the fragrance of spirits of air when summoned. In *Grimorium Verum*, it is said that the air has to be made clean and suitable for the appearance of a demon.

some did; however, they preferred to remain invisible for this reason and usually didn't reveal their presence or do anything. He leaned forward in a secretive manner and whispered, 'There are more jinns around than you think. Some may be observing a person all the time unknown to them, even when one is in bed with his wife; others may be living secretly in someone's house and they might never know. You can never tell why a jinn might decide to do something or the other. This can go on for generations, since jinns have very long lives and nothing untoward may happen in this time. Occasionally some small ghostly incident might take place, the kind people often relate. More rarely there may be serious episodes such as mysterious fires or disappearing children. Jinns can never be trusted.

'In very ancient times, which Hindus call the previous cycle, demons ruled the world. However, mythology relates how religious deities and heroes rid the world of these creatures.'

I couldn't help smiling at this and told him there was no geological or anthropological proof of this. 'There is definitive proof of the evolution of prehistoric man.'

He smiled in response. 'I told you about parallel worlds. When the cycle changes, there is a transition,' he explained and continued, 'It is very difficult to control jinns. Only the Prophet Hazrat Solomon could do it.'

Then he looked at me with sadness in his eyes. 'I'm sorry to tell you that only the demon who spirited your cousin away can tell you what it did with her. But you don't know who it is, and how will you find it in a parallel world? Often jinns who enter our world learn to speak our language, but even if you could somehow confront this jinn and speak to it, it will never tell you the truth,' he told me, patting my hand, before adding, 'There was a curse on your family. There is no doubt that your cousin is dead. The dream was only a construction of your imagination, picking up suggestions of danger in the future and presenting them in a manner that would create an impact on you.'

Before we left he gave me a strip of bark and told me I would be able to see the invisible world if I chewed on it. He was gracious enough not to charge me anything.

That evening we went to see a famous fortune teller. She was recommended by my mother. She was well known in society for being an accurate palm reader. At least she served us coffee and tasty snacks that she had prepared, so it wouldn't be a dead loss. Then she read my palm.

'I see a long life, one marriage and three children,' she told me, examining my hand.

Well, that was reassuring. It meant that I would survive the danger, whatever it was, if she was genuine.

'I see some trouble at the present time,' she told me, a bit alarmed.

This seemed accurate. 'What kind of trouble?' I asked, concerned.

'How can I tell? But it's not financial or romantic.'

She continued examining my palm. 'I see you going on a journey.'

'Well, that's news.'

'And I see you going on a second journey while you're on that journey.'

This was all I could find out that day. My main question remained unanswered: where should I look for Koyel?

Night was falling and a wintry mist of haze and smoke from the fires of poor people was silently gathering in the air. As we drove back I looked at the old, blackened with age, brick facade of Zeenat Mahal, venerable old trees towering around it in the growing darkness, and wondered what danger was drawing near.

~

The next evening Ijaz chacha came to visit us. My mother quickly sent for some patties and pastries from the shop right outside our house (one of those that had come up on the land I had sold) and there was Ijaz chacha's inevitable cake, so we had a sumptuous tea sitting in front of the log fire in the parlour. Our guest had got news of the state and had rushed over to tell us. Apparently the Indian government had abolished the stately unions and the position of the rajpramukh (governor of the union) but the allowances would continue to be paid to princelings. This meant that officially the state of Hashtpur had ceased to exist, not that it mattered to me at all, but I felt a strange sense of deprivation, if not loss. Anyway, that's that, so big deal.

'We better not tell Badi Baaji,' my mother said after he left.

'Not that she'd understand these politics. By the way, where is she?' I asked.

'She's upstairs. She's been searching for something all day.'

After that we discussed the day's events and the portentous danger.

'Beta, what are we going to do now?'

Just then we heard Badi Baaji shriek upstairs.

'Oh dear, don't tell me she's having another fit,' my mother said, perturbed. But the shriek was followed by ululating cries of elation. Then she came down the grand baroque staircase, almost dancing. She always wore the ornate, regal ghaghras she used to in the palace and the heavy silk swooshed on the steps.

'I've found it,' she announced triumphantly.

'What have you found, Baaji?'

'This,' she said, holding up a small gold pellet. 'I knew I had kept it somewhere.'

'What is that?'

'This is a piece of the nawab's taweez,' she told us. 'I secretly broke it off once because I thought it could come in handy one day. And now we need it!'

'Wow!' I thought. 'What an idea. If the whole thing protected our family from the curse, maybe a small bit would help too.'

'Will it work?' asked my mother. But Badi Baaji didn't answer.

'I've got an old ruby brooch. You can attach the pellet with some tape to the back of the brooch and wear it.'

'Will it work?' my mother asked again.

'Why not? If you believe in it.'

'Well, at least it's something,' my mother said, looking at the tiny trinket.

'Can't you see the emanations coming from it?'

'Frankly, no.'

'Try some of my medicine, then you might.'

'Your medicine gives me a headache,' the rani – sorry, ex-rani now – said wryly. 'Come, have tea. There's cake and pastries; Ijaz chacha was here,' she added, ushering her into the parlour.

'Oh good. I hope there are lemon tarts. He must have come to tell you that the old state does not exist any more,' she told us.

We were flabbergasted. For all her waffling and not knowing whether it was night or day, sometimes she displayed incredible insight.

'How do you know?' my mother asked, amazed.

'Shahji told me.'

'When and how, if I may ask?' my mother asked.

'In the dream I told you about. I thought about what else it could have meant when he handed Mehran beta the ruby that the nawab wore on his royal turban.'

~

That night I had to attend a mehndi function because Ammi was not feeling very well. She probably tried my grand-aunt's paan again. As a precaution, I wore both the hakeem's taweez and my grand-aunt's brooch, which made for a pretty smart tiepin, and looked like an heirloom. We shahzadas – sorry again, ex-shahzadas – are supposed to have a lot of heirlooms.

The father of the bride was a businessman known to my mother and the mehndi was held in the lawn of his big house in the up-and-coming housing society Gulberg. It was a very vibrant affair with a lot of singing, dancing and snacks. I joined some friends and we stood to one side joking and laughing and ogling the girls. I saw a couple enter, visibly very rich. The host seemed to be especially hospitable to them and sat them on a sofa in the front row. Something about the man caught my attention. He was impressive-looking, tall, and had long hair. The last time I had seen him his long hair had been wild and unkempt and he was wearing a decrepit black robe and a garland of beads. That was twelve years ago. Now he was well groomed and dressed in a smartly tailored suit made of imported material. Yes, he was the same amil who had exorcised that servant girl. At least he looked just like him; his features hardly seemed to have aged. I turned my attention to his wife, also well dressed, carefully coiffured, wearing tasteful jewellery and an expensive Indian sari. She was much younger than him and stunningly beautiful in a ravishing, feral way, but unbelievingly, I recognized her as well: she was the same servant girl who had been possessed. She had grown into a young woman. This was too much of a coincidence, I thought to myself. Had that fellow somehow come up in the world? Had he latched on to the girl he had exorcised? What with premonitions of danger, I wisely kept myself hidden from his sight. I moved a bit to the side so was hidden by the friend I was talking to. Then, as soon as I got the opportunity I surreptitiously walked over to Fakhr, the son of the host, and asked him who that person was.

'Mr Shamoon?' he said, gesturing towards the couple.

'Yes, yes. Don't look. They mustn't see me.'

'That's Mr and Mrs Shamoon. He's a prominent businessman in India who deals in jewellery. He's very rich. My father met him there and has business dealings with him. He's here on business and staying as our house guest.

'In fact, he hails from your kingdom. They say he's from a very modest background, a serf or religious figure or something, but now he's a multi-millionaire. Do you know him?'

'Well, I thought I recognized him. But it seems he's certainly doing well for himself.'

There was something suspicious here. I was dying to find out what exactly happened that night of the red moon and perhaps get some clues about Koyel. I strategically sat on one of the chairs directly behind Mr Shamoon. It was unlikely he'd look behind him, so I could observe all he said and did. Maybe I'd find out something. He appeared to be getting annoyed at his wife because she was keen to join the singing and dancing. Finally, with a deliberately sexy and rebellious wiggle of her hips that would annoy her husband, she marched to the centre where all the girls were sitting, singing. I could see the man glancing around a bit nervously, hoping no one had seen his wife's behaviour. The bride's sister welcomed her. She made her sit beside her and join the singing. The man watched disapprovingly. Then the girls began dancing. Mrs Shamoon was good. She moved her hands and limbs and gyrated like a professional dancer and when she did some small acrobatics and rolls the people were very impressed. The family requested her to perform solo. I watched, stunned by her performance and, of course, other attributes. Mr Shamoon got up in a huff and went into the house.

I was very curious. I continued watching for a while and then realized I wasn't going to learn anything like this. The only thing to do was to confront the exorcist and see what he could tell me. I went into the house. I knew my way around Fakhr's home. It was very big and the family lived on the ground floor. The upper floor was practically empty and unfurnished, except for the guest room, the passage and a few other rooms. When I reached the top of the stairs, I found that the passage was lit and the other rooms were in darkness. The newly painted doors and polished floors reflected the light.

The guest room door was closed. I knocked lightly. There was no reply. I knocked louder and called out, 'Mr Shamoon.' Still no reply. I tried the handle and the door opened. I called out his name again and peeked in. The room was dark. He was lying on the bed, much in the manner of a corpse, his body straight, facing upwards, hands folded on his chest. My entrance hadn't disturbed him.

'Excuse me, Mr Shamoon,' I said in a loud whisper and moved forward. Then in the light from the passage I saw that he was lying with his eyes wide open, looking straight up. He didn't turn to look at me or blink. The sight was creepy and unnerving. How could anyone sleep like that? He hadn't stirred even after I had called out to him; was he in a coma or something? Then it struck me that I was being very foolish. I was supposed to be in some danger. During the exorcism I remembered my grand-aunt saying, 'They are not what they seem.' I caught his somewhat ammonia-like odour and could almost sense the eerie vibes emanating from his body. 'Who is this Mr Shamoon, or rather, what is he?'

I was glad he hadn't woken up. I quickly left the room. Once I was back in the lighted passage, I quietly closed the door and was just starting to turn around when suddenly I heard a hissing snarl. Startled, I looked up and to my horror splayed flat against the roof and glaring down at me was his woman. The next moment she leapt down on me, her hands raised like talons; claws in place of nails. From playing polo my reflexes are quite good and I managed to crouch just in time to avoid the claws. I had to save myself from them at all costs as they could be poisonous. She landed on top of me and we fell to the ground. I quickly flung the pallu of her sari over her face and moved to one side, managing to avoid the slashes of her claws. With one hand she snatched the cloth off her face and with the other grabbed my lapel and banged me hard on the floor. She was incredibly fast and strong. But as she tried to grab my throat she suddenly recoiled. I guessed at once it was because of the taweez I was wearing. Despite her superhuman strength she was light, so I managed to throw her off, at least for a fraction of a second. Just as I was thanking my stars for the taweez, she ripped it off by the string and threw it aside with a distasteful grimace. She was too fast; as soon as I rose to my feet she grabbed me again and was about to claw me once more when for a fraction of a moment she recoiled in surprise seeing my grand-aunt's brooch. That split second helped me duck her slash again. She went at my face again and again at lightning speed, but I was able to duck each time. The next moment she grabbed my arm and threw me through the air right across the room. I hit the wall with dreadful force. However, I had taken falls from my horse and knew how to roll with the impact. My adrenaline didn't let me feel stunned and I turned and ran into one of the empty rooms and locked the door behind me. In two seconds she crashed through the door. However, my brain had gone into overdrive and I had the sense to stand next to the door on one side. When she dashed in, looking first towards the bathroom on the other side of the room I ran out, heading towards the stairs. In a flash she was in front of me again, blocking my way, snarling and glowering at me like a savage beast. She dived at me but because I knew exactly what she was going to do I managed to duck to one side and she couldn't grab me. I wouldn't be able to keep saving myself like this. Luckily, when she threw my taweez it didn't fall on the floor but landed on a side table that was right next to me now. I recalled how she had blanched when her body had touched my brooch, so in a reflex action I snatched the taweez and threw it at her. She baulked and grabbed at it when it hit her and that gave me the time I needed to dash past her and somersault over the railing of the stairs. Fortunately, the second flight of stairs was below me so the fall wasn't too great. I had the sense to hold on to the railing as I rolled over it, so when I released my hands my momentum was broken slightly. I didn't worry about how badly I was hurt when I hit the stairs below. Rolling and scrambling, I gathered myself at the foot of the steps, practically dived and made it out of the front door in one motion. As I ran down the drive, I could hear music and cheering from the tent. Apparently nobody had heard the screams and ruckus from the house. Terrified and with my heart pounding in my chest, I didn't stop for a moment and ran on to the road where my car was parked. Fortunately, Afsar was sleeping inside. I quickly shook him awake and we drove off as fast as we could. Panting and gasping, I told him what had happened. Now I felt my adrenaline backlash and collapsed on the seat.

'You should have shot them,' he said.

I didn't bother to refute him. Clearly the couple was not human. Now I began to feel the aches and pains from the bumps. My suit was ripped. I was lucky. It was a mehndi function so I had worn my second-best suit. Lucky? Ha! I should say, things could have been worse. And how! I had only been able to save myself because of my protective amulets. I had received two slight scratches. They were only skin-deep but they itched so much and had become so red I realized my fear of her claws being poisoned was correct. From horse riding I knew such minor scratches would not cause tetanus, so they should be safe from poison as well, I hoped.

I couldn't sleep all night, dreading that the couple had followed me home. Locked doors couldn't stop that tigress. I certainly wouldn't be able to survive a second attack by her. If I heard anything I could go hide, but then who knows, she might attack my mother and Badi Baaji. As I lay sleepless, wild and fearful thoughts kept going through my head, and suddenly the full implications of what my grand-aunt had said hit me. Shah sahib had presented the emblem of the nawab's rule, the ruby on his turban, to give to me! Yes, it fit. Just as the exorcist and that girl had been present for the curse in Hashtpur, they had shown up here. The question was how did the demon who ripped off my ancestors' heads perceive the curse? Did he see the realm as it was historically, or did he accept legal interpretations with regard to inheritance even after radical changes in the existence of the state? Now that the princely state was gone, the last bit of property left was Zeenat Mahal, and I was heir to that!

Well, there was still about a week for the full moon, which gave me some relief. Soon I drifted off to sleep.

4

In Thrall to the Curse

It was a cold, rainy morning. When I awoke I began to feel the pain from all my bruises. I hobbled down to the dining room for breakfast. My mother was surprised to see me in this condition.

'What happened to you?' she asked.

I told her all about my encounter. She listened wide-eyed and was very upset.

'Oh Meeru, thank heavens you're alive! What are these people? Where have they come from? Badi Baaji said they were evil. Are you sure you're all right? Should we see a doctor? You might have broken some bone.'

Then I told her about Badi Baaji's interpretation of the curse. Now she was very, very disturbed.

'Oh dear, it's true!' she uttered in distress. 'That horrible curse has caught us. Badi Baaji is always right about these things. Do you remember her dream that I told you about? And now this dreadful couple has come into our lives again. And have you noticed, recently there have been sunspots and a thin red halo around the moon? Oh Meeru, what will we do? What will we do? How can we escape the curse?'

'Don't worry, Mother. I managed to escape that female jinn, which means these demons are not infallible,' I assured her.

'Don't be foolish, beta. That was only because of the taweez and the brooch, and because you were lucky. We don't know what sort of creatures that exorcist and his woman are. But the real demon of the curse is bound to be much more powerful. We saw him that dreadful night, remember? The curse has already killed five of our ancestors and my niece. It's real, and without the nawab's taweez nobody can escape it,' she said, becoming more and more distressed.

'Please, Ammi, don't get upset. Nothing has happened and nothing will. Don't forget when Ghazala aunty read my hand she said I'd get married and lead a long life, which means everything will work out fine.' I tried to comfort her.

'Oh Meeru, she's only a palmist! A curse will always run its course. You can't stop it. There are only six days to the full moon. We can't possibly get that taweez. Even if there was time the shahzadi will never send it to us and in any case, according to Badi Baaji's dream, it is lost.

There's nothing anybody can do!' she said sadly, and it anguished me to see her look away and wipe her tears.

'Ammi, please don't cry. I'll be all right. Really, I know it,' I said, hugging her.

Well, I wasn't very scared of the curse, or rather not as much as the danger warranted. I don't know. To me it seemed like the inevitability of fate, and whether it was overconfidence or youthful conviction in my invincibility, I didn't feel fatalistic vibes. What I was frightened of was the real and present danger of that halfling (for that must be what he was, a human who had partially turned into a demon: half demon and half human) and his deadly companion. I didn't know what that creature wanted but my instinct told me he was after me and he might come to our house any time. My proximity to my mother could prove dangerous for her, so the first thing I had to do was to get her and Badi Baaji out of here. Perhaps I could take them to a hotel till this blew over. But in her present mood I couldn't even get her to finish her breakfast.

However, she seemed to feel less downcast as I comforted her. She patted me on the cheek and said, 'You're so naive, Meeru. But maybe there is something I can do.'

'What's that, Ammi jaan?'

'I don't know. Nothing is certain. It's a chance I have to take.'

But she didn't tell me what she was thinking and

when I suggested she and Badi Baaji go to a hotel for a few days she refused.

There was a lot to be done that day. I wanted to visit the hakeem, this time with my mother and Badi Baaji; maybe he could suggest something else. However, my mother said that first she had some other important work to attend to with our lawyer. She refused to tell me what urgent work had suddenly cropped up at this crucial time and kited off with the car. I thought it was necessary to do what I had planned but apparently she had her own priorities. What the heck! I'm supposed to be the master of the house and heir to what's left of Hashtpur, but mothers, even in history, have the power to overrule rulers. She came back at two o'clock, belatedly, according to me, because who knew what the night would bring and the days were getting short. I had a limited amount of time to consult the hakeem and try to find some sort of defence against a possible visit of that preternatural couple come nightfall.

So we set off as quickly as I could and took my mother and Badi Baaji to visit the hakeem. But he only gave us all one more taweez each. However, he recommended an old woman from Bengal who could come to our house and cast some protective spells by burning herbs. To me these seemed like facing tigers with an airgun.

We drove back to Zeenat Mahal. Our servant Ismail Khan opened the door for us and informed us that a visitor had showed up in our absence and asked for me. Ismail said he had never seen the tall, bearded, long-haired man before. He added that the stranger was accompanied by a woman who did not step out of the car. 'Maybe his daughter or wife. I couldn't tell because she was much younger than him.' I knew it! The halfling *was* after me. A few more details about the couple's appearance confirmed my suspicion. I thanked my lucky stars that we had not been at home. Now I didn't bother to convince my mother or listen to her objections: I just told her she had to go and stay at a hotel for a few nights and practically pushed her and Badi Baaji back into the car and told Afsar to drive off. I didn't even let them enter the house; he could be secretly waiting inside. We checked in at Needos hotel.

'Where are the mountains?' asked Baaji, looking out of the window. Since we were in a hotel she thought we must have travelled to a hill station.

I told them I would bring them their luggage later. My mother said I should stay with them in the hotel. In my present bedraggled condition, I was tempted to do so. If I had another run-in with that fearsome hellion I wouldn't stand a chance, no matter how many amulets I wore. And the hakeem hadn't come up with anything better. But on the other hand, I nursed a desire to try to find out what that creature wanted and what happened that night. I felt it was my fate to do so. Moreover, I didn't want him hunting for me all over Lahore, as that could lead him to my mother. I had to see this thing through and I would be better off doing it alone.

My mother insisted I stay and became quite emotional as mothers usually do in moments of crisis; they have this idea that their sons are helpless babes, even though they might be rated four goalies in polo.

'Don't worry, Ammi,' I assured her. 'I'll be all right. The hakeem gave me something with special powers,' I lied.

'What did he give you? You told me how deadly that female jinn was, with the strength of ten men and poisoned claws.'

'Ah! But at that time I didn't have this,' I said, showing her the piece of bark the hakeem had given me.

'What is that?'

'It is . . . it is a special bark the hakeem gave me that will make me invisible to demons.' I thought this was a stroke of genius I came up with on the spur of the moment.

'Make you invisible? What nonsense!'

'Not to humans, only to demons from a parallel world, like they make themselves invisible to us as he explained to you,' I said, adding another brilliant detail to make it more plausible. After all, this whole situation was quite fantastical.

'I don't believe you. He didn't give you anything like that in front of me.'

'He gave it to me the last time I visited him. He

guaranteed it would work. So, don't worry about me. If worst comes to worst, I'll make myself invisible.'

'You're making this up. Why didn't you tell me about this earlier?'

'No. It's true. Unbelievable as it sounds, this is what he gave me. I'd never lie about such an important matter to you, Ammi,' I told her, full of sincerity. I can be good at this sort of thing.

Well, that was how I managed to get away from the hotel. Then Afsar and I went to the Bengali crone and brought her home. The first thing I did was ask all the servants to leave the house and take seven days off. The full moon would have passed by then. I didn't want any of them falling victim to any jinns. I could fend for myself in this interim.

Then the Bengali woman cast her spells. She wandered from room to room with some smouldering, pungent-smelling herbs in an incense burner, mumbling incantations and scattering handfuls of different types of lentils about the place. It would be a devil of a job to clean up afterwards. Frankly, I didn't have much faith in this mumbo-jumbo. I had seen demons and what they could do in real life. Anyway, I ate the bark. It was so bitter I couldn't chew it properly. It made me feel very nauseous and I had to sit down. I almost fainted; however, the fit abated as quickly as it had descended on me. I looked around with a new clarity of vision, like someone who has just cleaned his glasses. I was half scared I'd see some demons. Of course, nothing of the sort happened, but the effect that the bark had on me made me feel that it had heightened my sight.

When the crone was done with her fumigation, Afsar and I went to drop her back. My main purpose was to give my mother and Badi Baaji their luggage, but I was also curious to see if I spotted any jinns on the way. I saw nothing and couldn't help wondering if this was a scam like the emperor's new clothes. It was dark by the time we got back – the dreaded night had fallen. I told Afsar to leave as well but he insisted on staying.

'No, I think you should leave. It might be dangerous for you to stay. This world can do without me but you are indispensable,' I joked.

'Don't worry, I've got this to protect myself,' he said, showing me his .45.

This spelt real trouble. Who knows what damage he'd do with his miniature cannon and still end up as jinn fodder. 'In that case you better leave.'

With difficulty I convinced him to remain in his quarters and not come into the house, no matter what he heard.

Then I went inside to face the night alone. Yes, I did feel scared. I felt like a general on the eve of a battle he was destined to lose. I decided on a strategy: I'd keep all the lights on. I'd stay in the upstairs portion and sleep in the storeroom at the end of the passage. I would lock my bedroom door so an outsider would think I was in there, and I'd keep the door of the storeroom wide open so nobody would suspect I was inside and it would also enable me to hear any sounds in the house and peek out if necessary. The moment I heard something, I'd run out to the servants' quarters at the back, climb down the stairs outside and look through the lighted windows to see what was going on in the house. I would have to stay awake.

I kept thinking of the narrow escape I had had the previous day. I don't know what impression you will form of me after reading this, but I'm only an adolescent; I've hardly touched a girl. The closest I've come to females has been to the mares I ride and I might say that sometimes I view their rounded haunches lasciviously. Therefore, even though I was feeling apprehensive I couldn't get over the physical contact I had had with a sexy dame and though she was some kind of dreadful demon and had been trying to kill me, I must admit I fantasized about her for several months after that.

Thus, the night passed. The house was absolutely silent. Lahore was also very quiet. In the distance I could hear a railway engine coming to a halt. Occasionally I'd hear a tonga clip-clop on the road beyond the tall trees of the drive, and for a while I heard the distant sound of the lion roaring in the zoo. I might have dozed off. Soon I felt very thirsty. The tension had made my mouth dry. The house was completely quiet, so I decided to quickly go to the dining room and get a drink of water. It seemed safe.

I descended the brightly lit staircase and couldn't help thinking that if the halfling was hiding somewhere he'd be able to see me clearly. The staircase was a grand affair. The front passage opened into a round hall two storeys high and a balcony with arches running around it. The balustrade had two ornate curved flights of steps going up on either side against the walls to a decorated large arch on top. When I was more than halfway down the stairs, I heard a sound from the balcony. I looked up and thought I saw something dash to one side. My heart sank. Only the jin'ni could have made the speedy motion that I had glimpsed. This was what I had been dreading. The halflings had somehow entered the house. Still looking up in fear, I pressed my back against the wall so that I would be less visible to someone up there. Then I looked down, and got the shock of my life. Mounting the steps right in front of me was the exorcist wearing a red robe. It seemed like certain death. He was hardly eight steps down, walking up purposefully, but it seemed he hadn't seen me. How was that possible? Why wasn't he looking at me? I just stared at him, now almost right next to me, and my eyes travelled to my arm outstretched against the wall, and wonder of wonders! I couldn't see anything. I looked down at myself and again I couldn't see anything. I raised my hands and looked up. Nothing. I was invisible! No wonder it appeared that the exorcist couldn't see me. It was a miracle. I had been lying when I said this to my mother, but it turned out to be true! The creature came so close I had to press myself back against the wall and hold my breath. I dared not make the slightest movement. I felt the full impact of his presence. He was gliding up the stairs, his gaze fixed ahead as if he didn't need to see where he was stepping. His eyes were full of malignant purpose and his body seemed to be sending out radiations, impalpable but I could feel their dire, overwhelming effect. To see the dreadful form move silently past me was one of the eeriest sensations I've felt.

His fearsome companion leaned over the railing of the balcony and spoke to him in the village dialect of my estate, which I had always had difficulty understanding. The bitch was wearing a low-cut dress and I could see the top of her breasts as she leaned. She spoke fast so I couldn't make out what she said. The exorcist replied in the same dialect. It seemed strange, somehow characteristic of our origin, seeing these terrible fiends talking like rural folk. I could make out they were searching for something. The exorcist said he could sense it was very close. 'He will have it on his person. Where is he?' he asked. I wished he would move along and cautiously started down the stairs, away from him. I breathed a sigh of relief when he went up to the balcony. They couldn't find me if they couldn't see me. It was crazy, but the alternative was certain death. I had reached the ground and the couple were up in the balcony when another startling thing happened. There was a flash of light and a burst of flame up there. The next moment the pair came down like a lightning flash. The woman dashed as fast as a cheetah and the man first appeared in one place, then in another with a blur like the images of a camera catching interspersed flashes when the motion is too fast for it to register. In a fraction of a second, they reached the partially open front door. I was determined they shouldn't get away unscathed. Heeding Afsar's dictum, I whipped out my pistol and shot at the halfling when he stopped momentarily to open the door. I got off two rounds and wisely dived to one side because the shots would reveal my position. I definitely hit him but the only effect it had was that he whipped around, raised his hand and the next moment a flaming bolt shot out right where I had been standing. I felt the sudden stream of searing heat as it passed and hit the railing with a loud impact. I was glad I had had the sense to duck. I realized that though I was invisible, my gun wasn't. I quickly threw it away and rolled to one side.

Fortunately, it seemed something had scared the creatures and the next second they were out of the house.

Slowly smoke from the two incendiary bolts began to gather in the enclosed vestibule. The next moment Afsar burst in flashing his .45. Suddenly I found I had become visible again.

'I heard shots! What happened? Where are they?' asked Afsar, looking around. I got up painfully, whooshing and moaning, and leaned on the staircase. Though these monsters hadn't got me, but the way I felt after the previous night I was convinced that the diving around would do the job.

'They came but somehow I drove them off. I can't understand what happened. I'll tell you once I get myself together,' I said.

'You should have shot them.'

'I did shoot him, twice. The bullets didn't affect him.'

'Well, maybe not a two-two, but a .45 will show him what's what,' Afsar said firmly. 'Where is this smoke coming from?' he asked. The railing was charred and part of it was smouldering. Afsar put it out with his hands, tough-guy style.

I sat down on the first step and asked him to check the balcony to make sure nothing had caught fire. He came back with a scorched runner and told me the marble had some burn marks. We checked the front door and found the creature had burnt the lock right off like a welder. This is how they were able get in so quietly and that hellion didn't have to break down the door.

Then I told Afsar about all that had happened and my miraculous escape that followed.

'Apparently the invisibility comes down like a cloak. I could almost feel it. It covered me completely, clothes and everything, but anything I picked up was still visible. I had no idea that the bark would have this effect. I can't believe it! I just made up the story to tell my mother that it would make me invisible to reassure her. I never dreamt it would actually work like that,' I explained.

'No, Mehran sahib, it was not the bark that made you invisible. The hakeem didn't mention anything like that. You said you couldn't see your hands or body but you were perfectly visible earlier when you ate it and also right now. Don't you realize that someone or something threw that fire bolt at the demons and scared them off? Don't you see what this is?'

'No, Afsar, what is it?' Well, I told you I wasn't too bright.

'Everything that you have told me, about becoming invisible and someone, rather something, throwing a fire bolt at them shows that some supernatural creature was protecting you. It made you invisible. Some demon has become your guardian angel. You have been incredibly lucky.'

'Good heavens! Is such a thing possible?'

'It's the only explanation.'

'Why didn't I see it? I've eaten that bark.'

'Perhaps it kept itself hidden from you.'

'Why should a demon do me such a favour?'

'Who knows? The hakeem said they are wilful, unpredictable creatures.'

Suddenly, like a revelation a thought struck me. 'It's Koyel! She's alive somewhere in the world of demons and sent one to help me.'

~

I was ecstatic. The thought that Koyel was alive, watching me, filled me with happiness and my heart was singing with joy. But why hadn't she contacted me? Why had she remained quiet for twelve years? Was she a prisoner in the parallel world? How did she get there? Could she see or hear me? A thousand questions crossed my mind including, 'Was I merely being delusional?'

Well, now I knew that the exorcist was searching for something I had. I couldn't imagine what it could be but I had something he wanted, which meant maybe I could bargain with him. All I had to do was phone Fakhr and talk to the halfling. That would also ensure he wouldn't come around and try to kill me again. After all, how much could I rely on my mysterious guardian angel? He had done me one favour, would he stand by me again? Let's say that was something I wouldn't bet my life on, and unfortunately that's what was on stake.

There were too many risky, unknown factors in this scheme. Thus, I was undecided. Two days passed. Now

Afsar slept in the house in one of the spare rooms near the kitchen which used to be reserved for visiting subjects from the state. Frankly, I was glad for it. However, I dreaded to think what he would do with that revolver of his if those halflings came again. He would probably shoot all the windowpanes and ornaments in the room and no doubt I'd end up as collateral damage before the creatures got him. Besides, I wished he would wash his socks more often. I wasn't certain if the demon would come to save me again in case of an emergency, but even if it did have a soft spot for me and decided to help me, for all I knew it might just leave the mahal after getting a whiff of Afsar's socks. During this time we ate food from the stalls outside, and the hours passed slowly.

On several occasions I picked up the phone to dial Fakhr but put it down each time. How could I be certain that the halfling would react rationally? It was too risky. I was too scared of that fiendish duo, sexy lamia notwithstanding. Soon the initial euphoria of a possible breakthrough in contacting Koyel passed. I realized I was still where I was when I had the vision that night. It might be another ten years before there was another such visitation or it might never happen at all. Perhaps my conviction that she was alive was only wishful thinking after all. However, the more I thought about it the more certain I became that I was correct. She was alive, somewhere unknown. All the other victims of the curse had been decapitated, but

Koyel had suddenly disappeared. Clearly there was something different here. I had to find out exactly what had happened.

There was no other option but to talk to Fakhr.

'You've got some gall calling me.'

'Why? What are you so annoyed about?'

'After what you did on the night of the mehndi, I should have you arrested.'

'I don't know what you're talking about. I didn't do anything,' I said, my mind racing to think of what Fakhr could possibly have heard about my encounter that night.

'Don't act so innocent. You broke down my door. You didn't even bother to apologize afterwards.'

Of course, that! 'What door? I don't know anything about any door,' I said quickly. I told you I was good at this sort of thing.

'Did you or did you not go and see Mr Shamoon after he went into the house during the mehndi?'

'Well, yes, I did. But he was sleeping, so I left.'

'Oh really? Then who broke down the door!?' he asked angrily.

I certainly couldn't tell him that Mr Shamoon's lissome wife had done that. Nor could I tell him that his house guests were supernatural fiends.

'I told you I don't know anything about any door,' I repeated. 'Besides, do you think I have the strength to knock down a door?'

'Oh, I know you and your tough polo friends; boisterous, spoilt brats, each one of you throwing tantrums and fighting always. You have no regard for other people's property.' He snorted and continued accusingly, 'Mr Shamoon told me you visited him that night to discuss some very old matter. You sat together and talked. You were drunk. Then you got angry and broke down the door in a fit of rage. Do you deny that?'

'Fakhr, I don't drink, at least not much. This is all nonsense. I told you, he was sleeping and I left.' Best policy: stick to your alibi under all circumstances. I learnt that in school.

'Well, you and your mother didn't come to the other functions, which proves you are guilty.'

'My mother's illness got worse. We couldn't.' Under all circumstances.

'Some of the drivers said they saw you running out of the house and you left in a hurry that night.'

'Oh!' This was a poser. 'Er . . . I had to go to the bathroom.'

'Then next time stick your head into the WC and keep it there!' he shouted and banged down the phone.

This was a problem, but I had to talk to this Mr Shamoon. I dialled again.

'Listen, I don't want to talk to you,' Fakhr said angrily.

'Please, Fakhr. Don't hang up. I swear I didn't break your door. Believe me. But since you're so upset, send me the bill for repairs. Okay? Now I've got to talk to Mr Shamoon, please. It's important.'

'You want to speak to Mr Shamoon after all that?'

'Yes! It's very important.'

There was a pause, and then he said, 'I'm sorry. He left yesterday. He's gone back to India.'

So that was that. I had hesitated too long.

~

Feeling depressed I went to the roof that night to play my flute. I looked at the moon. The asymmetric luminous disc certainly had a reddish halo. The situation was turning more and more hopeless. I sat in the moonlight and played with deep sadness. I was completely engrossed in my music when an instinct made me glance over my shoulder. There was a dark shadow sitting there. A chill ran down my spine. I realized that a not-unpleasant odour I had been smelling, like that of scented old clothes, was not coming from outside but from whatever was sitting close behind me. Timorously I began to turn around to look.

'Oh! You can see me,' said a rasping, whispering voice near my ear. 'Don't turn around. You'll get scared.'

My heart jumped. I was terrified. I didn't know if I should try to run or what, but somehow it didn't seem all that unexpected. I gasped when I felt a hand on my shoulder. It was extraordinarily hot.

'Don't run away. Continue playing. I like it,' the hoarse, sibilant voice said again.

'Who are you?' I asked.

'Must you know? My name will be meaningless to you.'

'Will you harm me?' I asked nervously.

'I'm not allowed to.'

'Who doesn't allow you?'

'The inner spirit.'

'What is that?'

'I don't know. It's just there. It's always there.'

'You always do what this inner spirit tells you?'

'I do whatever I want to. Nobody tells me what to do,' he hissed vehemently. 'Come on, play some more. I want to hear more melodic sounds.'

I could sense the hot alien presence right next to me.

'I can't. I'm too scared. Wait a moment and let me calm down a bit.'

Then a thought occurred to me.

'Are you the demon who saved me the night before last?'

'Yes, from that unspeakable mongrel and his woman.'

I felt his hot breath on the side of my face.

'Why did you do that?' I asked, hoping, dearly hoping, to hear what I wanted to hear.

'You play beautiful music.'

I was disappointed, but I felt safe. It was so strange – here I was talking to a dreadful demon while through the trees of the drive I could see the lights in the shops and people walking by and attending to their daily routines. Then I asked him, 'Do you happen to know a girl named Koyel?'

'Sounds human. Why? Should I know this girl?'

Maybe I should be more specific. 'You know there's a curse on my family?'

'Yes. Everybody knows that.'

'Ten years ago, a demon came and spirited her away because of that curse.'

'Well, then she's dead and gone.'

'But a few nights ago, she suddenly appeared before me. It wasn't a dream. I swear she was alive. It was like the visitation of a ghost except she was there in flesh and blood, very much alive. The next moment she disappeared. I want to find her. Maybe she's somewhere in your demon world. Can you tell me how I can find her?'

'Is it because of her that your music has so much sadness?' he asked in a softer tone.

'Yes.'

There was silence. The lull after the fear I had been feeling suddenly made me aware of how beautiful the night was. There were a myriad stars in the sky and I caught a pleasant hint of the aroma of night flowers.

After a while the demon said, 'Maybe you can find some information in Sikkinsala. That is the fortress where our ancestors sleep. It is in the mountains far away.'

'Where is it? What mountains?'

'The high mountains. You can reach it through Semphel Dom of the Shengshong by the Dodoka wall of skulls near the town of Nakchu.'

'The Semphel Dom of the Shengshong? What is that?'

'It is a Buddhist monastery far away. But no human has ever entered the fortress in thousands of years, as far as I know. Anyone who enters the fort cannot return.'

Well, at last I had some sort of clue.

'Thank you . . . er . . . what is your name?'

'Hishoo.'

'Thank you, Hishoo. My name is Mehran.'

'I know.' Then after a pause he added, 'But you will never be able to go there.'

'Why do you say that?'

'Because in two days the demon of the curse is coming for you.'

I played some more for him, my mood different now.

~

Hishoo told me he couldn't help me because Dajaar Galakara, the demon of the curse, was much too powerful. I waited for the full moon like a prisoner on death row for the black warrant. Each night I looked at the moon. It was almost completely round the night after I had the encounter with the demon. But some aberration in the atmosphere made it hard for me to focus on it. It cast a slight double image that enhanced an effect like a red halo around it. A red moon could very well follow, at least partially. I suppose that could count. The next night it was raining and I couldn't see the moon because of the clouds. I went to sleep feeling disappointed, but awoke around midnight. I quickly wrapped a shawl around myself and went outside. There were only a few clouds and the sky was so clear that it looked dark even with the silvery, almost full moon that shone mysteriously. There was not a hint of red in it. Was it possible? Did this mean that the curse wouldn't fall? I really didn't know what to make of it. The moon could very well become red the next night. Who knows. Or maybe we'd have a red moon the next month. I had heard so much about the ineluctability of the curse that I had become quite fatalistic.

The following morning I went to the hotel and met my mother. She too had noticed the moon. She was very hopeful. But she's an incurable optimistic. She only sees the good side of things – of people, events and how things are going to turn out. She is more concerned about being upset by a problem rather than the problem itself. Indeed, we've seen many difficulties in our time but she's always remained blissfully oblivious of adversity even in the maw of misfortune. However, I felt encouraged by her attitude, though we parted with a long emotional farewell.

Night fell. The moon was clear. I was alive the next morning, with my head still on my neck. Early at fajr Ammi phoned me to check if everything was all right and we both were overjoyed. So much for the curse, I concluded cynically. Well, that threat seemed to have fizzled out and the halfling appeared to have returned to wherever he had come from, so we were safe again. Afsar and I went to pick up Ammi and Badi Baaji and bring them home. As we drove back, Afsar looked into the mirror and commented, 'That's odd.'

'What is, Afsar?'

'When we left the mahal this morning, I saw this blue Oldsmobile and now it's behind us again.'

But everything seemed all right at that moment and I didn't bother about what Afsar said.

Life at Zeenat Mahal returned to normal once again, except now I had a new trail to follow. I had difficulty figuring out where Nakchu or Semphel Dom was. I did something I had never ever done before. I consulted an encyclopaedia, which told me Nakchu was a town on the extreme west of Tibet and Semphel Dom was a small monastery in the Shengshong ruins near Nakchu. I also learnt of an ancient aerial burial ground called Dodoka which means 'the wall of skulls'. The burial custom of Tibet in the olden days was to preserve the skulls of the dead. Shengshong was the first kingdom in Tibet that ruled around 900 BCE and this place had been the centre of the primeval religion of Bon, which I learnt was similar to Buddhism and also amalgamated folk beliefs. You can see I learnt a lot. I must say encyclopaedias can be very helpful.

But during those few days something was making me uneasy and I couldn't put my finger on it. Well, for the first time I had faced real danger and that had made me feel very insecure, apart from confusing me sexually. I was jumping at shadows. One night, however, I think my wariness was well founded. I had to go to the medical shop outside the mahal. On the outer part of our driveway, there are a lot of tall trees and shrubbery with a high hedge behind them. Beyond that is the street, lined with lamp posts. Naturally, the light filters in through the foliage, and as I walked towards the gate that night I thought I saw a shadow in the bushes. The next moment it seemed to have disappeared. I began to feel that I was being watched.

Well, one can't let unconfirmed qualms disrupt one's routine or divert one from what is important. I applied for a Tibetan visa. In those days, for most countries, you got a visa when you landed, but Tibet, though ostensibly an independent country with the Dalai Lama as its ruler, was under Chinese influence. I contacted Nawabzada Shamsher Ali, an old family friend who had been the scion of a neighbouring princely estate before Partition. He had settled in Lahore. He was a very important person with contacts in the government and had also been appointed as an ambassador once. He advised me not to travel to Tibet as it was going through a veritable civil war, apart from the fact that no one went there in winter. However, on my insistence, he said he would make the necessary arrangements.

It was quite a rigmarole. I had to state I was a scholar – big joke – and the purpose of my visit was to study the Shengshong civilization. Uncle Shamsher had clout and got me the visa in two days. I went to his house to collect it from him, along with my ticket.

'By the way, just recently I met another old durbari of your uncle from when he was the nawab,' he told me after handing me the documents. 'An interesting fellow. He used to be a poor mendicant but now he's a multi-millionaire. What was his name – ah! Mr Shamoon.'

'Mr Shamoon!?' I exclaimed. 'Tall, red beard, striking eyes?'

'Yes, that's right. You know him?'

'We've met. Recently, you mentioned? Can you tell me when you met him?'

'Just three days ago. He was in a bit of trouble. He had overstayed his entry permit and asked me to get him clearance so he could leave.'

'Did you get him the clearance? Do you know if he's left?' I asked anxiously, my fears returning.

'Yes, he left yesterday. Charming wife he's got.'

'Yes, absolutely killing,' I replied.

~

So Fakhr had lied. The halfling must have told him to. And probably my suspicions of being watched weren't nerves after all. Thank heavens he didn't attack us again. Hishoo must have really scared him off. And I was more thankful now that he had finally left.

During this interim, the mystery of the curse deepened. Three days after the full moon night Ijaz chacha visited us. He was very sad and told us that the old shahzadi had died. It was believed some dacoits had sneaked into her bedroom and killed her during the night. They were so cruel that they cut off her head.

'It's strange but it's as if the curse got her.'

We commiserated with him and sent our condolences to the shahzadi's sons. But I couldn't stop thinking that actually it was the curse and somehow it had killed her instead of me.

A few days later, this mystery was solved. The mailman delivered a registered package from our lawyer. It contained some legal documents that had been completed and registered. I glanced through them and couldn't make out what they were – they referred to the old court case the shahzadi had filed against us and what puzzled me was that it had her name as the legal owner of Zeenat Mahal. I asked my mother what this meant and she quickly took the papers from me, saying, 'Never mind. Never mind.' She can be quite a sphinx at times. She hid the papers away and knowing her, I would never be able to find them. However, I discovered what this was all about when later that day Falek Sher, our lawyer, called to ask if we had received the documents. So I checked with him about them. Apparently, Ammi had gone to the court and nominated the shahzadi as heir to Zeenat Mahal. She had referred to the old claim the shahzadi had made on this estate. That case had been decided in our favour ex parte because the shahzadi stopped following up on it. Now my mother had given a sworn statement in front of a magistrate acknowledging the shahzadi's claim to be correct and conceding her right as owner of the property. She said that she had been under a misconception that the nawab had given Zeenat Mahal to her when she contested the shahzadi's claim. Later she found out about her mistake, therefore she had rescinded her claim on this property and acknowledged the shahzadi's right of ownership. Thereafter, the ex-claimant had been advised by mail that she was the owner of the property.

I was left speechless. I asked if this meant we would be evicted. He said that if the shahzadi had decided to follow up on her claim, she would have applied for a court order to be given possession of the mahal, and I could have filed an appeal against it. He pointed that we had been in possession of the house for over twelve years, so we already had administrative rights and our case was very strong. 'Anyway, I believe the lady passed away a few days ago.'

He added, 'I made sure your mother's statement had no legal basis whatsoever. I don't know why she decided to take such an unwise step. I felt I had to protect her interests despite herself. So I was careful that nowhere in her statement did she in any way gift or give the property away to the shahzadi. That would have strengthened the shahzadi's right to evict us. She only conceded her rights and acknowledged the shahzadi's claim, giving no proof whatsoever apart from her verbal and unverifiable statement, whereas in the old case documentary proof of her ownership had been presented in court and was unchallenged. Thus, if worst came to worse and you took the matter to court, you would have a strong claim. I have never heard of such a case before, where a client has no legal reason to rescind their claim, yet does so.'

Well, who could have believed it? My poor, docile mother had achieved the impossible and saved me from the curse. Since she wasn't the owner of the property and the shahzadi had become the beneficiary from the date she filed her claim, when Zeenat Mahal became what was left of Hashtpur, she became the ill-fated heir. You can think what you like about my mother, but in all fairness I must say that she was unsure her scheme would work. She was just desperate to save her son. Moreover, she had probably forgiven the slights and deprivations of the shahzadi a long time ago, so there were no vindictive feelings. I couldn't help wondering about that haughty and callous shahzadi, who in her heyday had oppressed my mother and insulted her in so many ways. She could never have dreamt that this quiet, submissive woman, who accepted the way she treated her with forbearance, would one day be the instrument of her undoing.

5

Appointment in Shangri-La

It was very cold when I landed in Patna. From there I took a connecting flight to Tibet. As we flew over vast snow-clad mountains, I realized it was one of the most dramatic flights of my life. Often the DC-3 had to navigate the rugged slopes, and more than once I found the rocky escarpments just a few wing lengths away. I reached the newly built Damxung airport in the evening. Built at an elevation of over 4000 metres, it was one of the highest air terminals in the world. It was freezing and the cold air hit me as soon as I stepped out of the aircraft. From the airport it was a short drive to Lhasa, once known as the Forbidden City, but later becoming a great tourist destination. Subsequently the trouble had started.

It hadn't snowed yet and the drive was very scenic,

with neat rows of spruce and poplar trees lining the road and terraced slopes stretching away to the silent mountains. Everywhere I found evidence of a dual culture. There was the old, feudal, Buddhist way of life on the one hand and communist propaganda posters on the other. The older part of the city had cobbled streets, narrow lanes and wooden buildings in the traditional Tibetan style and other parts were spacious with signs of some modern civic structures and government offices. Posters all over warned people not to spread rumours or indulge in political activity and there were checkposts manned by Chinese soldiers. The people seemed quiet and surly. But the Chinese interventions were not necessarily negative. Among other things they had constructed the new Damxung airport and the highway on which I drove. I was headed to the hotel where I would spend the night.

I better confess that I didn't tell my mother where I was going. She'd think it was dangerous and get worried. I told her I was going with the polo team to play in Gilgit. She had heard of the Shandur festival.

'During winter?' she asked, surprised.

'You've heard of winter sports, haven't you?' I replied quickly, true to form.

The hotel turned out to be quite comfortable. The next morning I found the mountain air fresh, exhilarating and nicely chilly. Uncle Shamsher had arranged for me to meet a lama from an important monastery. He was very courteous and gave me a letter of recommendation for the Nakchu monastery. He told me to be careful. There were guerrillas fighting in the countryside but with the onset of winter it would probably be safe for me to travel to Nakchu.

There were no longer any tourist tours. I had to catch a ramshackle bus, full of rustic Sherpas, to get to Nakchu. The bus slowly rattled up the precipitous road, passing vast patches of snow and breathtaking views of unbelievably expansive mountain ranges. The Sheng Shong ruins were perched on top of a high mound and behind them was a beetling massif. Everything was covered with snow and it was a hard walk up to a small red-roofed monastery on one side of the ruins. I knocked and a monk bade me enter. He was wearing spectacles and sitting in a chair reading a newspaper in a nice warm room heated by a metal brazier. I greeted him and gave my letter to him. He seemed to know a little English. He read the letter and asked what he could do for me.

'I want to go to the fortress of Sikkinsala,' I told him.

He looked surprised. 'Nobody but a few of us have ever heard about the fortress of Sikkinsala. It is a closely guarded secret of our elders. Who are you that know of this fabled fortress and say you want to go there?' he asked, looking at me intently.

'I am a man whose beloved was taken away by a demon,' I replied and added, 'I am very serious.'

Then I told him about the curse and the visitation.

'Verily that is a place of asuras. But frankly if an asura has taken your beloved and many years have passed since this incident, it is hard to imagine that she would still be alive,' he said sombrely and then added, 'But if you have had a visitation, real or imaginary, there must be some meaning to it. I will see what we can do.'

He sat me down, offered me hot tea and some thick dough biscuits and then went into the back room. Soon he came back with his companions, one of whom was old and venerable with a long white beard.

'This is our guru, the honourable Yarsen Xungzhu. He is wise with years and knowledge. He is the only one among us who knows anything about Sikkinsala.'

All the monks bowed to me, including the old one. I quickly bowed back. Then the guru began to narrate something in a sing-song tone, looking straight ahead, as the bespectacled monk translated what he was saying.

'The Sikkinsala palace was built many thousands of years ago in the highest mountains in a region that overlaps the world of asuras. It is not visible to human eyes or machines. It was built by King Shamanitsu, who had attained the tenth dana paramisi of complete enlightenment. Buddhism is much older than you think. There were seven Buddhas before Sakyamuni. You see, Buddha is not only a person; it is a state of mind. Compassion is creation, to give the gift of life and care for it. This area used to be ruled by asuras. Shamanitsu built Sikkinsala guarded by four yatuviras, one on each corner. These yatuviras are dreadful and wrathful giants; Shamanitsu endowed them with special powers. They watch over the palace. However, asuras were allowed to seek sanctuary there and rest in the underground caverns or return to their world since Sikkinsala is a portal through which they can come and go. Later in the time of the evil Mongol king Jeemanshi, who used asuras to conquer the world, Sikkinsala became the abode of asuras. Such are the ways of Fate. The fortress that was originally meant for one purpose later became an outpost for the exact opposite cause. For a long time jinns roamed the land. Thousands of years later Padmasambhava, of the lotus born, drove the asuras out of Tibet. Since then, as far as we know, no human has ever gone to Sikkinsala. There is supposed to be an army of asuras sleeping in the underground caverns there, and when they awake they will rise again and conquer the world. That is why we keep the existence of the citadel a secret. However, according to legend, only an individual who is meant to go there will be able to find the way and make the perilous journey.'

Then the guru beckoned me to the window and looked out at the cliff towering behind the monastery. He pointed to it and asked me something.

'He asks, what do you see?' my translator told me.

I looked out and all I could see was the high rocky face with snow-rimmed crags. But even as I looked I began to discern with greater and greater clarity stone stairs covered with snow carved into the rocks, going up the cliff in a criss-cross pattern and circling out of sight around the top.

'I see steps leading to the top,' I told him. The spectacled monk translated it for the guru.

He nodded sagely and said something to my translator.

'He says that love is the essence of the first Brahma vitara, which is maitri, and can only be attained by pure emotion. It is your love that enables you to see the path. We will help you go on this journey.'

Then everyone except my translator went into the other room. They took so long I began to think they were not going to return. But they came back, the sage holding an ancient cylindrical scroll container. He took out a very old scroll of silk that had yellowed with age, opened it on the table and read it carefully, his finger following the script. Then he looked up and spoke, the translator relating what he said.

'It is a long and dangerous journey. You will have to climb these steps you see to wherever they will lead, beyond the eagle's flight. Then you will come to the gate of stars. Inside you will find a sword. You will have to take that because an ordinary sword can't defend you from the dangers that lie ahead.'

'Well, I brought along this,' I said, showing them the two-two pistol that I had carried with me for the expedition.

'Please put it away,' the translator said distastefully. The monks were averse to such weapons and violence. 'These toys of bloodshed shoot normal metal. They will not avail you where you are going.'

'Beyond the gate is the Sky Bridge. It is better if you spend the night in the gatehouse and start crossing the bridge in the morning, because it is very long.'

'How long?'

'Around ten miles. On the way you will have to pass through tunnels, where bhasakalas* will be hiding in the darkness. They will attack you.'

'What are bhasakalas?'

'They are giant evil birds, predators, much bigger than eagles. You will have to carry a light and fight them off with the sword.'

'Oh,' I said uneasily, regretting that I had given up my fencing lessons.

'In Sikkinsala you will be attended to by a mountain preta. A preta is a phantom who eats humans. But don't be frightened, he is the caretaker that Shamanitsu ordered to look after the guests. He was taught to speak human languages. He doesn't dare go against what Shamanitsu commanded, even after thousands of years. He is scared of the yatuviras. Food for the guests is brought by dhakanas, imp-like creatures who are overtly harmless but their mischief can sometimes cause great

---

*Whereas the other creatures are adapted from Buddhist lore, this creature is merely an imaginary creation.

damage. Occasionally ro langs serve the guests; they are like zombies of children and young people. These are the servants of the palace and they keep the preta well fed. Thus ordinarily he will not be a danger to you.' I certainly didn't like the sound of that.

Then I took my leave of them. There was much bowing between us again. It seemed the monks as a rule couldn't be polite or humble enough, but I felt they were now genuinely interested in me and liked me, and were also concerned about me. First I returned to Nakchu to buy the equipment I would need. Since the place was popular with mountain climbers, it had a store where I found what I needed. I also bought a helmet with a powerful light, the kind used by spelunkers. If I could I would have bought a rocket launcher as well.

Early the next morning I set out again for the Nakchu monastery. I found all the monks waiting for me. As I went out of the back door towards the cliff, the guru spoke to me in a serious tone. The translator explained, 'My guru says you may chance upon strange sights and sounds in Sikkinsala. It is a dangerous place for humans. He advises you to do whatever you have to do quickly and get out of there as soon as possible.'

'I assure you I will,' I replied.

'By the way, what do you intend to do there?' he asked me.

'Sir, I really have no idea.'

~

They say a journey of many miles begins with a single step. Well, this adage certainly doesn't specify how difficult the subsequent steps will be. My journey of many miles was straight up. The steps were supposed to be thousands of years old so initially I tested each one with my alpenstock, but I guess what is built by magic is maintained by magic even after thousands of years. The steps were narrow and had no railing. The higher I went, the more nervous I became. All the monks stood below watching my progress. Each time I looked down they bowed towards me. Soon I could only wave back to them, because with the narrow steps and rucksack on my back my bow would be 200 feet downwards. Finally, exhausted and panting for breath, I reached the turn on top of the cliff. And what do I find? The trail continued steeply up another mountain, but at least now it was a clear track. Thus, I continued slowly, going higher and higher. Sometimes there were steps, sometimes a path. I had to cross one or two high altitude rope bridges, which would terrify me normally, but with rope railings to hold on to and after the precarious steps I had traversed I found these to be relatively easy, though at one point I was practically paralysed by fear, stuck on the precipitous steps in the middle of a huge cliff face like a minuscule speck. The immensity of the mountains was unbelievable and all along my trek there were breathtaking vistas. It was a land that was cold, hostile and beautiful in its awesomeness. Looking at the clouds and the myriad, mighty snow-clad peaks stretching out infinitely, I felt I was on the roof of the world. Finally, by late afternoon I reached a large and ornate Chinese gate. It was a gatehouse with rooms and windows above the entrance. I breathed a sigh of relief.

I tromped down the snow-covered slope and entered the shelter of the wide roof of the gate. On one side was an ornate door with a dragon motif. I opened it and found stairs leading to the chamber above. It was a pleasant room, with beds and resting places surrounding a fireplace that was a sunken square in the centre, typically Tibetan. The back wall was a fancy Chinese trellis with two openings on either side, one that went into a small kitchen area and the other to a small storeroom. The bright beams of the setting sun streaming in through the line of windows behind me – brighter in the clear, rarefied mountain air – made the scene look hospitable and pleasant. I immediately looked around for the sword the guru had told me about, my Rajput blood keen on acquiring that traditional weapon. Once I had it in my hand I would at least stand a chance against the demons. I found the sword on the other side of the trellis in a third chamber, and sure enough it was magical because it hung suspended in mid-air. Behind it on the wall was its decorated scabbard, a spear and a shield. It was a scimitar and indeed it was very beautiful, with an ornate, jewelled knob at the back and a similar larger one in front of the handle. The blade was slender, slightly curved, gracefully widening at the end to two points. I would feel like some legendary hero wandering in this strange land with this beautiful magical sword in my hand. I tried the trellis and part of it slid open. I went in and reached for the sword. Something very strange happened. The sword shifted to one side. I tried to grab it again and it shifted to the other side. I scrabbled for it but it kept eluding my grasp as if it was alive. My first reaction was one of deep disappointment. Everything here was magical. The way only I could see the path because I was meant to, perhaps the sword was dodging me because I wasn't supposed to have it. What the heck! It was right in front of me. How long could it escape me? I snatched and grabbed at it again and again and it kept evading my hand successfully. If anybody was looking, I would present quite a comical spectacle. I was getting very frustrated. I needed that sword. The guru said it would be there for me. Then another thought occurred to me. I told you I have a keen sense of smell. The room smelled like other mountain rooms in Tibet, of fresh air and damp wood, but there was a feisty, somewhat organic, odour in the air as well and it was stronger in this cubicle. I stepped back and took out the hakeem's bark from my pocket and chewed on some of it. After the initial bout of befuddlement, I tried to focus my eyes. Sure enough I saw two imp-like creatures. I guessed they must be the dhakanas. One was standing there holding the sword and it was he who was moving it when I was trying to grasp it. The other one, who was quite fat, was standing to one side and they were both grinning, covering their mouths and silently laughing at the sport they were having with me. It wasn't magic that levitated the sword. When I stepped forward, the rascal got ready to dodge the weapon again. He didn't know that I could see him now. I just strode up and gave him a kick on his backside. The creature yelped, dropped the sword and ran past me before I could kick him again, but the fatter one wasn't so agile. He looked dumbfounded and I kicked him twice before he dashed away. I quickly took the sword and other armaments and looked around, feeling satisfied. Having eaten the bark I could see things that I couldn't before. I looked up and saw a horrible spider one foot wide, crawling in a corner of the roof. I noticed something slithering down the chain of the lantern hanging in the room and what appeared to be an enormous centipede at the entrance of the storeroom. The place was infested with huge creepy-crawlies! I was lucky I hadn't been bitten already. Terrified, I dashed out as quickly as I could. I went down the steps and ran out of the gate. I wasn't going to stay here in a million years. Well, I found some shelter beside a rock. I had a blanket in my rucksack. So sleeping on part of it and wrapping what I could of the rest around me, I slept in the open. It was freezing, but the day's weariness made me fall asleep soon. The sky was incredibly starry and beautiful.

~

I awoke early in the morning, covered with snow but feeling surprisingly fresh. The previous day's exertion had toned all my muscles. I then set off again, this time armed with the magical sword. The effect of the bark would last a couple of days. I had figured out that I could get my normal vision or invisible sighting whenever I wanted to. All I needed was to blink my eyes with a hard squinch and that would alter my eyesight from one mode to the other. When I got to the gatehouse I ran through it to avoid the creepy-crawlies. Beyond it was an amazing sight – a stone bridge starting from the high mountains I was on, spanning the incredibly vast and deep valley below, stretching away and disappearing from view towards the distant mountain range on the other side. It was of a comfortable width so I began to walk over it. I was surrounded by majestic snow-capped mountains covered by clouds. The only sound was the whistling high-speed wind.

The bridge went on and on. I had to stop several times to rest. One has less stamina in rarefied air. The stupendous vistas soon lost all their beauty for me. The mountains below gradually became higher and higher as I approached the range on the opposite side; soon the bridge had to twist and turn around the mountainous terrain like an emaciated and suspended version of the Great Wall. As it began to get dark, I passed through a craggy cleft and reached a tunnel. I switched on the light on my helmet and entered with great trepidation, the sword in my right hand and the shield on my other arm. Now I knew I had to be careful not only of the dreadful birds the guru had described but also of huge insects. It was a very creepy place that got creepier as I went in further. It stank of something dead. The roof and walls weren't brick-laid but had been carved out of the rocks and the protrusions caused the light from my helmet to cast long shadows. At many places there were pitch-dark niches that could be hiding anything. The roof was overhung with cobwebs. I felt more and more apprehensive as I went along. This land of magical wonders had a very sinister undertone. I stepped on something squishy that squirmed and uttered a shrill, clicking noise. I got worried about the tunnel being miles long like the bridge. But soon I spied a light far away at the end, though I must have already walked a mile by now. Then on the dark roof my light fell on some shadows that seemed to be leathery folds. I realized it must be one of the birds. It was stationary. 'It's probably sleeping,' I thought, and with my heart in my mouth I passed it warily. I kept looking back towards it and only when I was some distance away did I start concentrating on going faster towards the light in the distance. Suddenly I heard a swoosh and a metallic clacking sound behind me. I wheeled around, swinging my sword in the same motion. The bird was very close to me and the sword was so sharp it cut off part of its beak and head in one stroke. The next instant there was a fluttering sound in front. I spun around, raising my shield. Another bird was flying straight at me and banged against it, knocking me down. But I got it with two strokes even as I fell. However, right behind was one more. The light seemed to dazzle it a bit and I was more ready for this one, though I was sitting on the ground. I managed to divert its long beak with my shield and sliced its head right off the neck. I had to heave myself out from under its body. In a panic I ran, wanting to get out of this horrible tunnel as soon as possible.

Once outside I was still scared the birds might come flying out. But I suppose they only emerged at night. Soon I came upon another tunnel and it took all my courage and willpower for me to enter it. My knees shook uncontrollably after the fright I had had. A little into the tunnel my heart stopped when I saw another shadowy form hanging from the roof, but this bhasakala quickly flapped its wings and flew away from me. Maybe now they knew who I was. Fortunately, this tunnel wasn't nearly as long as the previous one and I got through it as fast as I could. More encounters with those predators and I might not fare so well.

Later, when the sun had descended behind the

mountains, I topped a high ridge and in front of me I saw a magnificent Tibetan citadel perched on a steep hill. On each corner, towering above the wooden lattice lining the top of the wall of the fortress was a huge figure, almost as tall as the wall itself. Each of them was dressed in a suit of Chinese armour of a different colour – dark green, carmine, dull yellow and brown. These were the yatuviras. They stood completely still and could be mistaken for statues, except when one got closer and saw that the hair and eyes were unmistakably real.

This was the fabled Sikkinsala, built by magic thousands of years ago, and I had at last reached it. I entered a small door set in a wooden frame at the bottom of the steep hill. A staircase had been carved in the rock inside the hill. I guessed it led to the citadel on the top so I began climbing the steps. The stairwell was lit by torches. I walked with the sword ready in my hand, prepared for anything. The windows were thin slits chiselled into the rock and the wind whistled through them eerily. Soon I reached an anteroom with a large embellished wooden door. Now I was at the ground level of the fortress. As I looked in through the entrance I saw a dark, shadowy passage lit by a single brazier with small wooden doors on either side. Then my eyes fell on a figure coming down the galley towards me. He was dressed in a cowl.

'Greetings, human,' he said to me in Hindi. 'I am your host, the keeper of this sanctuary.'

The figure was gaunt, very tall and I couldn't see a head inside the cowl.

'Greetings, oh keeper of Sikkinsala,' I replied.

'What do you want?' he asked. He spoke in a whispering, hissing tone, unused to articulation.

'A place to rest for a day or two.'

'Our custom is not to refuse anyone. You are welcome, human.'

He showed me into a spacious room with a door opening into the veranda along the courtyard. It was very well decorated in the old Tibetan style with carved black wooden pillars and beams. A coal fire was burning in the sunken fireplace in the centre. A brazier hanging from the roof bathed the centre of the room in a dim, wavering light. The eerie figure made a gesture with his hand indicating to make myself comfortable. The hand was white and wizened.

'We have toilets and hammams with hot water for humans. They are by the north parapet.'

A large tray of food floated in as if by itself, but when I squinched my eyes I saw that a dhakana was holding it. The poor creature was dressed in rags and the exposed parts of its body showed bruises from being beaten.

'Eat, human,' the figure sibilated without any emotion in his voice.

'Thank you,' I said, accepting the plate proffered by what would seem an invisible hand. I decided to keep my ability to see these creatures a secret from the preta.

My enigmatic host kept standing and I realized he was observing etiquette and waiting to be dismissed.

'Please sir, I wonder if you could help me?' I said, and told him about the purpose of my visit.

The figure stood quietly and for a moment I thought perhaps he had not registered my query. The short interlude made me realize how completely silent the citadel was, the only sound being the wind whistling with a moan through the passages of the old building.

Then the figure spoke. 'I know not how I can help you. True, Dajaar Galakara would have come and gone through here and an entry to that effect would have been made by the sequencer of names. The sequencer registers every creature that passes through. You could consult it, perhaps it might tell you something. But the archives lie beyond the underground caverns and that is not a place for humans to go to.'

'I would like to go there if you could guide me,' I said with quiet determination.

'In keeping with the hospitality of this palace I cannot refuse you. But be warned, it is not a safe journey. We will see what the morrow brings.'

'By the way,' I said, unable to contain my curiosity, 'am I the first human to have come here in two thousand years?'

Again I was met with a pregnant silence. After a while he replied enigmatically, 'There have been others, very few, and even fewer have returned.'

The figure turned around and walked out of the room. A gust of cold air hit me when he opened the door. The dhakana lifted a pitcher of water to help me wash my hands. When the figure left, I turned to the imp and told him, 'It's all right. I can wash my own hands.'

'Sire, you can see me?' it asked, frightened.

'Yes, don't worry, I won't hurt you. Have you eaten?'

The creature was encouraged. 'No, sire.' It looked hungrily at the food.

'Well, help yourself,' I said.

At once the creature began gobbling the food ravenously. For its diminutive size, it certainly had a big appetite, and after I washed my hands – by the way, in keeping with the impeccable service of the place, the water was nice and hot – I was lucky I could get a few bites before the dhakana finished it all.

Then the creature turned to me with pleading eyes and begged me to allow him to spend the night in my room. He was desperate and scared.

'Please, sire. Let me sleep here. I won't disturb you. I'll just settle in a corner. Please don't send me out.'

'Okay. What's the matter? Are you scared?'

'Sire, Dumaadra the demon is arriving tonight. He is one of the most powerful demons in the agnidesh. He is coming on the orders of the aryabharu to kill a hundred errant demons who have escaped to your world. The last time he was here he attacked the scullery. It took the yatuviras an hour to get him under control and he ate several of my kin in that time. He can see us even when we are invisible. There is no escaping him. Please don't send me there tonight, sire.'

'Don't worry. You can sleep here. And if this demon tries any tricks with me, I've got this,' I said, showing him the sword. 'I've already killed a dozen bhasakalas in the tunnels.' Well, three or twelve, not much of a difference.

'Sire, Dumaadra is so powerful the sword will be like a toothpick to him.'

I let the imp sleep near the fire on my blanket and covered him with my expensive fur coat. I lay down on the raised dais which was the bed and pulled the quilt – which was magnificent; made of silk with a dragon design on it – over myself. The hospice certainly treated its visitors regally.

'Perhaps this place is just too darned hospitable,' I thought wryly, feeling a bit uneasy, wondering how safe other visitors here were from such dreadful demons who took nocturnal carnivorous liberties.

Sometime during the night I suddenly woke up. Something dire and frightening had intruded my dream, almost turning it into a nightmare. It's only a dream, I told myself. The bed was warm and the quilt felt nice and I was very tired after the strenuous day. But some inner sense prevented me from going back to sleep. The sense of fear in my dream had been too strong. And it had definitely come from outside; it was not a product of my mind. I lay there in the dark, every faculty alert, listening to the wind moaning outside. The slight thump of snow falling from the eaves sounded very loud in the silence and practically made me jump up and grab my sword. I wondered what the time was. It was too dark to look at my watch. The room had a square line of skylights around the chimney in the centre of the roof and I could see the moon shining through it. It had that more silvery quietness that indicated it was declining, so it must be very late. The moonlight filled the room and I saw that the dhakana was also up. But he was cringing, hiding behind a pillar looking fearfully towards the door. Then I heard it.

It was a fearsome, bestial bellow that seemed to emanate from some deep chasm rather than from someone's throat. I sat listening intently. Soon I heard the sound of ponderous thumps coming from the veranda outside, like something extremely heavy and sluggish dragging itself along. The sound got steadily louder, as it came closer. Clearly it was something monstrous and of incredible bulk. Soon I could hear its long, deep and sonorous breaths. Each time it exhaled the expiration scraped a guttural growl in its throat. And then to my horror, it seemed to have stopped outside my door. I sat frozen in terror. The door chain seemed a miserably frail safeguard to hold the door and the door itself like a mere matchbox in the face of whatever was outside. Filled with intense fear I could practically feel my nightmare come alive. I could even feel it look towards my door. For a moment nothing happened. Every second seemed like infinity and I expected the horror to come crashing in any moment. But then I heard some running, a shrill shriek, and the heavy movement of that creature suddenly and surprisingly galvanized into cumbrously rapid mobility. There were bangs and crashes followed by desperate screams of the poor creature who had shrieked earlier. I could tell that the creature had moved away from the door, so I quickly ran to it and peeked out. In the moonlight I saw a towering hulk, a humanoid figure with a thick tail curled up like a scorpion's, stuffing a diminutive creature, probably a dhakana, into its mouth. But the very next moment, fast, heavy footsteps shook the ground. Strident, almost metallic, voices shouted something in Tibetan and soon huge shadows rushed forward. Terrified, I closed the door. Sounds of a monstrous struggle made the skylights rattle; there was screaming and confusion all around, before the heavy footsteps seemed to move away and the silence rushed back.

My dhakana came up to me warily, still quivering in fear. 'Poor Peelu. The creature got him,' he said sadly. 'Thanks be to kismet, the yatuviras caught the demon in time and took him away, otherwise we would have been next.'

I was relieved the drama was over. No doubt Shaminitsu's guardians knew their job and they'd lock that thing up somewhere safe. However, I suspected that according to the rules of the house he'd still be treated regally and not chastised or executed. I also realized why so few humans returned alive from Sikkinsala. Well, I was as safe as I could ever be in this place, so once my heart stopped thumping I'd try to go back to sleep.

Early the next morning, when the sky was still grey, the caretaker knocked on my door. I opened the door and he stepped in and looked around.

'The dishes haven't been removed?' he hissed, somewhat vehemently.

My instinct told me to cover up about my kindness to the dhakana and not let him know I could see the creature.

'Yes, I had my dinner late. I had some drinks first.' I told you I was good at this sort of thing. I looked nervously to where the imp was sleeping. That area was dark in the morning twilight and it just looked like I had flung my fur coat on the ground there. 'Your invisible thingamabob must have spirited away,' I commented.

The hooded figure stood there looking at me. I wondered if he could read minds.

'You didn't see any strange creature hiding in here?' he asked after a while. The dhakanas couldn't maintain invisibility while they slept. It was freezing cold outside and the taciturn thing just stood there at the open door least bothered.

'No! What sort of creature? There was some horrible commotion outside during the night. Something got killed, I think. What happened?' I responded, shivering from top to toe.

'My duty is only to care for the guests. Other problems are dealt with by the guardians. You have to be careful, human. This is an abode of asuras.'

Once he left, I quickly locked the door. When I turned around, I found the dhakana standing there. He was awake and must have seen and heard everything. The poor creature hugged my legs at once.

'Thank you! Oh, thank you, kind sir!' he said, crying in gratitude. 'You have saved me from a horrible punishment. I would have probably lost my tail. And last night you most definitely saved my life. Earlier there were awful screams coming from the scullery but you were sleeping so soundly that you didn't wake up. That horrid demon attacked the scullery and I dread to think that it must have killed many of my kinfolk. If I had been there, I would have been one of them. The good thing is that most likely the caretaker thinks I'm dead, so I can sneak out of this awful place and be free once again. I'll be free, manusya! Do you realize, I'll be free! Thanks to you. You are indeed a dhanbodhi!' he said excitedly.

'Hush! Keep your voice down. I don't want to get into trouble with that thing. But you can't leave before you've had breakfast, so wait a while and remain invisible,' I said, quickly going back to my bed and getting under the quilt.

'By the way, my name is Mehran, but call me Meeru. What's yours?' I asked, poking my head out.

He blushed. 'My name is Srotampapabalakamdha samanjamakoravabela-champigana. But call me Sru.'

In the morning, I went to the toilets the preta had told me about. They formed a line of cubicles behind the main pavilion and I couldn't help wondering that they were too many in number for an establishment that probably gets one or two human guests in a thousand years, but of course, they must have been built during Shaminitsu's period. As a precaution, I wore my grand-aunt's brooch and carried my sword wherever I went. Afterwards I wanted to freshen up with a hot shower in the hammam. I noticed that one cubicle was occupied. There were sounds of splashing and steam rising from the open slits on top. I was surprised. Demons don't bathe with water. There must be another human guest staying here. The bather hadn't closed the cubicle door properly and it was slightly ajar. I was filled with curiosity. What sort of person could it be? Could I sneak a peek without being noticed? The cubicle was filled with steam and the naked figure's back was towards me. Surprisingly, it looked like a boy, small and slight, but too big to be a dhakana. There was something ineffably attractive, smooth and curvaceous about the form. I noticed it had longish hair and when the person turned more to the side to reach the soap, its face more or less hidden by its hair, I saw alabaster breasts, immaculately shaped like those of a Greek statue. I realized it wasn't a boy but a woman; an undoubtedly beautiful young woman. For a moment I was gripped with intense excitement. This strange land was filled with all sorts of surprises, good, bad and fantastic. Fortunately, she hadn't noticed me yet. I suddenly felt like a peeping Tom and I certainly didn't want to start off on the wrong foot with whoever she was, so I quickly tore my eyes off her and went and hid behind a pillar in the pavilion nearby. I was just in time, for she emerged a short while later wearing a thick bathrobe with a hood, and again I couldn't see her face. I wondered which room she was staying in. All the ones lining the courtyard had seemed dark and empty. She didn't head in that direction. Instead, she took the stairs of the parapet to the level below. I followed at a safe distance to remain unseen. I wanted to find out where she was staying.

The stairs led to a lengthy alcove-like balcony with a carved wooden railing along the outer wall of the citadel. The woman was nowhere to be seen. She must have turned the corner at the end. I started walking quickly across the balcony in order not to lose her. Suddenly I heard a loud buzzing and the next moment I saw a swarm of huge bees heading towards me, each one about four inches long. I happened to be using my invisibility vision or I would have never seen them. My situation was hopeless. They were obviously lethal, small targets and too many. How could I save myself? Like a samurai warrior slashing impossible targets with unerring aim, I desperately struck this way and that, getting two or three that were in the lead. The next moment a miraculous thing happened. Suddenly the blade of my sword blazed up in flame, and when I swept it across it not only killed the bees near it but deterred the others from flying forward. It was indeed a wondrous, magical weapon. In a few seconds, the swarm flew away.

My next thought was to look for the woman. The poor thing must have been bitten by those fatal hornets because they had come from the direction she had disappeared in. I ran to the end of the balcony, turned the corner but she was nowhere to be seen. There was a closed door to one side and on the roof of this neglected nook of the citadel was an old, huge bees' nest. There was a hairbrush lying on the floor. The bees around the nest seemed very agitated, as if something had riled them, so I beat a hasty retreat.

This incident set me wondering. The sinister citadel was full of perils and mysteries. After I had caught my breath and calmed myself down, I went back to my room and got the shock of my life. The dhakana was standing there, holding something in his hands.

'Sire, I've brought a present for you.'

And he handed me the nawab's taweez.

6

A Hades Full of Demons

Sru explained to me what had happened. Soon after I had left, a strange man had entered the room. He had opened the latch from outside using a metal rod. He was tall and had a red beard. He didn't see the dhakana because he was invisible. He searched the whole room for something and apparently didn't find what he was looking for. When he left, Sru followed him. He was staying in another room to one side of the courtyard. When he entered his room he looked around, seemingly anxious about something, and then left his room again. The mischievous imp took this opportunity to rummage through the room and that's where he found the taweez. He stole it to give it to me. I didn't need any prompting to guess that this strange man was none other than Mr Shamoon. By some coincidence he was also staying here at Sikkinsala. He must have robbed the talisman twelve years ago in the confusion that had ensued after Koyel was spirited away on the night of the red moon. So that's where it had disappeared to. Now I had got it back miraculously thanks to this little rascal. I realized that it must have been the halfling's wife that was bathing in the hammam this morning. The whole thing was a set-up to kill me. She must have seen me going to the cubicles in the morning and then decided to take a bath in one of the hammams, deliberately leaving the door ajar to tempt me to follow her, thus eventually leading me to the bees. Probably she devised this plan on the spur of the moment and preferred not to attack me herself because I had a magic sword. If I didn't have invisibility vision and that scimitar, I would be lying swollen up and dead on that balcony right now. Ooh! What a diabolical plot. You see, I might be a bit slow, but I'm not dumb.

I thanked Sru profusely and if he hadn't been so goblin-like, with hard creases on his face due to exposure to the freezing cold, I would have picked him up and kissed him. I told him that this necklace belonged to my family and that half-baked demon had robbed it many years ago. I informed him that he was some kind of semi-demon and had a wife who had similar powers. Sru hadn't stolen the jewel; he had returned it to its rightful owners. I also told him about my other run-ins with this fiend where he and his woman had tried to kill me; how even this morning his wife had made an attempt on my life and I had had a narrow escape. 'What an unfortunate coincidence he's here at the same time I am.'

The dhakana's brow creased further and he looked serious.

'I tell you, manusya, it's no coincidence. Probably he followed you here. After all, very few people from the world ever come here; though this creature has been here before, I've seen him. The way he was looking around told me he was after something you have. It's important for him and that's why he's after you. Do you know what it is?'

'I really don't know,' I said. Now that I had the taweez I removed the small pendant from my grand-aunt's brooch and put it back in the taweez to make it whole again. 'I wonder what it could be,' I said, completely at a loss about what it could be that the halfling was looking for.

Anyway, what that imp had told me sounded correct. I must say the fellow was clever, probably almost as clever as me.

'Manusya, you must be very careful. That creature will guess you've got the taweez somehow and now he'll become desperate and try harder to kill you.'

'You're right, Sru. I better wear this taweez all the time. And you, too, be careful. Remain invisible and leave as soon as possible,' I told him, putting on the taweez.

'My large friend, I will leave, but later. Right now you are in great danger. I must stay and protect you.'

'Oh, don't worry about me. I can take care of myself.'

Unfortunately, I had left the door unlocked, and the next moment it burst open. The halfling stood there with his woman and before I knew it, he flung a dreadful bolt of fire at me. The flames seemed to hit an invisible shield just inches from my face. I guessed at once that the taweez was protecting me. He flung one fireball after another at me, but they couldn't harm me. I looked anxiously to see if Sru was all right, but he had the sense to move away from me. I grabbed my sword and surprisingly the hilt was cool, though now the pillars had caught fire. The woman shrieked and dashed at me full of fury. I had just enough time to turn the sword towards her and it pierced right through her abdomen. 'Oh nuts!' I thought. The halfling cried out and ran forward to grab her as she fell. I stood riveted, shocked at what I had done.

The next moment heavy footsteps shook the floor and immense shadows darkened the veranda. Using his hands, one of the yatuviras sent out cloud-like pastel-coloured tendrils that encircled the halfling, who was still holding the fallen woman, and carried them away. Another guardian looked in and with a powerful breath blew out the fire, knocking me over. It also blew the smoke out of the room.

'Oooh! That was fun. Well done! Well done!' Sru cried, jumping about and clapping his hands. I was feeling distraught and overwhelmed by the suddenness of what had happened. I really wished the rascal would shut up, despite the fact that it was he who had saved my life. I couldn't help thinking that I had put on the amulet in the nick of time. He did shut up the next second, suddenly covering his mouth and ducking back into a corner because he saw the caretaker walking up to the room. Fortunately, the imp still maintained his invisibility.

My heart sank. The creepy entity must have heard the commotion. I didn't know what he would say or do. I had slain a guest and my room was wrecked. Well, I had the sword to defend myself, that is if it could protect me against the creature. He was a ghost after all.

He stood silently at the door, looking at the mess. The beautiful quilt was also burnt. The carvings on the pillars were charred and blistered. Everything was still smouldering. There was a pool of blood on the floor.

'I didn't mean to kill that woman. She attacked me. Those two guests attacked me,' I blurted out. 'I didn't do all this–'

'We can go to the archives whenever you are ready, human,' he said in his cold, sibilant manner.

'Oh!' I uttered, understanding the situation. Of course, this was all part of the way things happened here. The hospitality of the place mustn't falter.

'Is there a doctor? Will somebody see to the woman?' I asked anxiously.

'If she is alive the sone will see her,' the caretaker

told me in a flat tone.

'Who is this sone?' I asked.

'Sones are evil witches but they know how to heal people, and this particular sone was ordered by the mighty Shaminitsu to attend to any accidents that might happen here.'

'Okay, thanks. But give me half an hour and we'll go. I'm very upset,' I told him.

'You may sit and have breakfast in the courtyard till your room gets fixed. The ro langs will serve you,' he told me, again gesturing outside with his pale, shrivelled hand.

Spindly, boyish creatures were setting out an easy chair, a parasol, a table and laying food on it in the courtyard. Apparently ro langs couldn't become invisible, though I wish they could or that at least I couldn't see them. Their faces were half covered by mould. I guessed after Dumaadra's visit last night there must be a shortage of dhakanas in the kitchen.

The creature turned around and left, and I noticed that an aura of cold air also seemed to dissipate. The sun in the courtyard was very bright and warming in the chill of the fresh mountain air.

~

Sru, remaining invisible, joined me for breakfast. When he heard where I was going, he wanted to come with me.

'You'll need my help, manusya. You will have to pass through the asura quarters. Then you will have to cross the Sea of Shadows. There will be untold dangers. And the ancestors sleep on the shore. Who can say when one may wake up. They are the ancestors; your charm won't protect you against them.'

'Have you been to this place?' I asked.

'No, but my grandfather has. He served the sequencer for a while. He told me all about it.'

'No, Sru. You'll just be a burden. I can take care of myself,' I assured him. I was still not over how I had swiped the bees in the air like a veritable ninja. 'Anyway, it's dangerous for you. Dumaadra is down there. Your invisibility won't help you. You better leave. This is your chance to get out of here while the caretaker is busy with me.'

He cocked his head, shrugged and left. Of course, I was a bit saddened at his departure, but it was for his own good. I guess I would never see him again. It saddened me somewhat because I had developed a liking for the innocuous rascal.

After breakfast the caretaker led me down the stone steps carved inside the promontory on which the palace was located. When we reached the bottom of the stairs we turned around an alcove, and in front of me was a very large gate carved out of the rock, with another staircase going down. From the cavernous depths below a ruddy effulgence rose up. We descended the steps. We kept going lower and lower as if into the deepest pit of the mountains outside. Dreadful sounds could be heard from the chasm below occasionally because the slightest noise reverberated and got amplified. Surprisingly the temperature kept getting warmer and warmer till it became quite hot. I suppose there must be something volcanic here. My expensive fur coat was beginning to feel uncomfortable and I had to take it off. It was cumbersome to carry. The caretaker asked me to leave it in a niche in the wall.

'It will be here when you return; if you return,' he sibilated cryptically.

'Thanks, that's very reassuring,' I replied, my sarcasm lost on my insensible host. The steps led to an enormous cave with several huge iron braziers. The dancing flames lighted the rocky nooks and crannies but they hardly illuminated the towering stalagmites and stalactites and cathedral-like immensity of the cavern. The place was like a scene from Hades, with shadowy craggy structures all around and a fiery glow. There were several open pits on one side and a phosphorescent radiance emanated from some of them, while others were covered in darkness.

'These are the quarters of our asura guests,' the creature told me in his hissing voice as he pointed at the pits. 'Though we have had very few humans visiting us in the upper chambers through millenniums, there are always one or two asuras here. I would advise you to be silent.'

I was glad when we left this place behind. Then we came to more steps leading further down.

'Now we will come to the fabled Sea of Shadows. Please remain as quiet as possible.'

At the bottom of the steps was the exit to the cave that opened out on a sort of flat natural quay, with turgid water in front and a cliff on one side. The enclosed area was better lit with flaming torches and the light from the large opening we had exited spread out on to this natural pier. The air here, with the hint of a gentle breeze, was different from that in the claustrophobic tunnels.

I could smell the murky water. There was a coral boat moored to the pier. The cowled figure began to pull in the rope of the boat. It got stuck on some obstacle underwater and the caretaker just kept pulling mechanically to free it. I strolled a bit further down the rocky strand below the cliff to see if I could kick it free. I happened to look up and my blood ran cold. About ten feet above, standing in an alcove in the cliff like a silent statue, was a form. He was tall, almost twice the height of a man. He appeared like a black mass at first; if darkness were to glow it would look like this. I discerned a slight grey vaguely outlining a figure of exaggerated proportions, the face completely dark. I could see the hint of a misshapen face, glowing skeleton-like teeth and slanting eyes. In the shadows I could make out wisps of scraggly hair. The figure emitted eeriness. This must be one of the demon ancestors, I concluded. He just stood there like a pagan idol and made me feel very uneasy. About ten yards further down there was another niche and I discerned a hint of colour. Out of morbid curiosity I went to see it. This large figure was wearing an orange fur girdle with several belts. He appeared in chiaroscuro from the flickering shadows of the torch. He towered ape-like just one yard from me. In his hand he held a huge axe. His visage was almost entirely just a large mouth; a fierce, fanged gash arced downwards, encircled by horrible leathery folds that made up the features of the face that also formed the bulging, glaring eyes. I gathered that these fiendish titans slept with their eyes open. I really felt he would reach out and grab me any moment.

'Don't go near the asuras, human, I advise you,' the caretaker hissed at me.

I quickly moved away. These weren't statues; they were alive and only in some sort of hibernating sleep.

My guide had got the boat free by now. We clambered in and he began rowing. Then we crossed the corner of the cliff and I saw the Sea of Shadows. The place was an unbelievably enormous cavern, the roof of which was like a dark sky stretching away into the distance above us. The expanse of water was literally a sea, a boundless, underground sea and I could not see the far sides. I was reminded of Coleridge's poem:

In Xanadu did Kublai Khan,
A stately pleasure dome decree,
Where Alf the sacred river ran,
Through caverns measureless to man,
Down to a sunless sea.

There was a twilight radiance along the horizon. Behind me the escarpment of the cliff continued for miles and miles and in the dim light I could discern the row of countless dark niches stretching away as far as the eye could see. I knew that each niche contained a nightmare beyond human ken, sleeping, waiting. The water was thick, black and oily. Who knows what lurked therein. The caretaker rowed slowly, like some Charon crossing the Styx. The only sound was the dipping and splash of his oars. There was no lapping of the waves in these subterranean waters. The cavern was silent; the silence of distance and immensity where slight sounds echoed and reverberated up to get lost in the starless sky.

I saw we were headed for an island some distance away. There seemed to be a ruined structure on it and a slight light was visible through a window. It would take hours to complete the journey. I just wanted to get out of this awful place as soon as possible. I had bad vibes about the whole place; the dark water, the distant black niches, the creepy island to which we were headed and most of all, I had bad vibes about the cowled figure rowing the boat. In my heart I dearly hoped I would find out something about Koyel on that island, or at least learn that she was alive somewhere, somehow. A dusty memory rekindled itself in my heart. I remembered how lovely the touch of a little girl's hand had felt while we played and that awakened a yearning I didn't dare allow myself to feel completely.

On the floor I found a bundle of small cylinders. I picked one up and looked at it.

'What is this?' I asked the caretaker. It looked like a firecracker.

'This place has untold dangers. That is your defence against the dangers here,' he susurrated.

'What can protect us against any of those guys sleeping out there? Or from anything that might lurk in these waters?'

'You are right, human, nothing can protect us from those. These only offer respite. They diffuse a dazzling light that will temporarily blind anything.'

'Oh! They're like flares,' I said. 'How do you use them?' I should know; in this place I might need to use one.

'It is magic. You hold it in your hand, close your eyes tightly and say the words "Akundasula abhijavahal!"'

Finally we reached the island. We hauled the boat ashore. Then the caretaker pulled a bell rope outside a building that was half in ruins. The door opened as if by an invisible hand and this was genuine magic since I couldn't see anyone there. Inside was a large hall of rough stone that was brightly lit. On a large wooden chair behind an old table sat a completely blackened, mummified figure looking at us as we entered. I gathered this must be the sequencer. With its stick-like arm and bony fingers it gestured us to sit. I sat but the caretaker remained standing.

'Oh sequencer! This is our human guest sent by love and fate. He desires to know of the visit of a certain demon,' he told him.

For a change I actually felt grateful towards my creepy host.

'Speak, manusya. What do you wish to know?' His voice was deep and hollow.

I said I wanted to know about the visit of Dajaar Galakara and gave the date of that fateful night.

The mummy was holding what looked like a rosary in his hand and began to sift the beads with his skeletal fingers. This went on for several minutes as the rosary was quite long, and I became more and more anxious. Finally, he stopped.

'Ah! Prince Mehran, your asura came to Sikkinsala two days before the date you gave. He came at the command of an impassioned curse uttered at the time of death of an ancestor of yours, a curse that was accepted by the old ones and ordained for all time. The asura captured the soul of a young girl on the night of the red moon.'

'He captured the soul of a young girl,' I repeated, my heart sinking. 'You mean he killed her?'

'Of course. A human is a shade without its soul.'

'Wait. Why didn't he behead the girl as the curse ordained?' I asked, hoping to find a loophole.

'I cannot answer that,' the mummy replied. His voice echoed in his throat. 'Only the asura himself can tell you that,' he continued. 'For some reason the asura didn't return afterwards. He is still in your world. You will have to ask him yourself.'

'Can you tell me where he is?' I asked, clutching at straws.

'He is in your ruined palace in Hashtpur.'

~

I came out feeling very downhearted. It didn't seem right. It wasn't fair. I had crossed over to another dimension; I had faced and overcome untold dangers just to hear this! Fate had led me here, preserved me. I was ordained to succeed. Could the sequencer be wrong? It didn't seem likely. These weren't humans. They didn't lie and detract. They may be frightening and cold-blooded, but they acted according to a definite code. However, my heart told me I was right. Despite everything I knew, I had faith that Koyel was alive and waiting for me. My teachers might have told me I was not very bright, but the good thing about being slow was that I believed I was right even if logic or facts indicated to the contrary. My feelings were in turmoil as we left. The caretaker slowly rowed us back. I looked at the dark, still water and had half a mind to throw myself in and drown.

We were still some distance from the quay when I heard a horn blow in the distance, across the sea. It was a very mournful and alien sound. I heard it again. I looked up at the caretaker to ask him what it was. However, just as I raised my head the figure suddenly vanished into thin air. Good heavens! Well, ghosts are supposed to have the ability to dematerialize any time. But why had it done that and left me out here? This didn't seem to be in keeping with its behaviour so far. I began to get very bad vibes and when I heard that dreary sound a third time, I felt scared. Slowly it dawned on me that some awful danger must be imminent. That's why the preta had left. That horn was calling to someone or something. I quickly went across the boat and picked up the oars to row. There was silence all around. I rowed for all I was worth, but the boat moved too slowly and the light of the pier was still far away.

Then I heard the water bubbling. In the dim twilight glow I noticed some disturbance in the water about two hundred yards away. I began rowing even faster, giving up the idea of heading for the pier. Now I just wanted to reach a shoal that was not too far away, but my plan was thwarted when out of the water rose a dreadful creature, like a sea monster, but I saw that his head was completely covered in metallic scales, which also covered his neck, talon-like forearms and sides and back. The scales glinted like hard, impenetrable metal and slid and shifted over one another with complete mobility, in sync with the movements of the creature. I immediately grabbed one of the cylinders. In my haste I had to repeat the incantation twice and I had the good sense to close my eyes, though I could hardly take them off the leviathan. The next moment there was a brilliant flash of light. Boy, maritime flares were nothing compared to these magical ones. When I opened my eyes it took me a second or so to focus them, but the flare had certainly stunned the monster and he remained stationary, partly out of the water. I resumed rowing the boat, desperately trying to reach the shoal. The creature recovered in a few moments and slid back into the water. It approached me like a torpedo. Very soon it was next to the boat and I could see the metal plates glinting and moving on its back.

It was a flesh-and-blood creature and my amulet couldn't protect me from a physical attack. I took out my sword. I would have to stand and fight, which wasn't easy with the rocking of the boat. I struck again and again on his back; the metal clanged and rang and the hardness jolted my hand, and try as I might I couldn't penetrate the armour. However, my trusty blade did have some effect on it and whenever I hit there was an immense spurt of sparks and the sound of an electric crackle. The monster did seem to jerk and recoil but I couldn't really harm him. He moved away a bit, then curled around and came for me from the front. But I was ready for him, and when he raised his monstrous head and tried to grab me with his mouth, I beat him off with my sword. He snapped at me repeatedly. Desperately, I kept swinging the sword at him. It was all I could do with the small, round boat rocking and swaying. I didn't bother keeping my balance or worry about the boat capsizing, and concentrated on watching the lunges of that horrible head as I smited it many times over. Had it not been for the sides of the boat, I would have tumbled into the water. Sparks and crackling lightning flashed all around and there were loud electronic bangs. Teetering and tottering and desperately slashing away, I knew I couldn't last longer than a few more moments. I wanted to take out one of the flares, but it was impossible for me to turn my attention away for even a fraction of a second. The monster tried to grab me with one of his frog-like talons, but rolling around I saw him coming and swung at him. This part of his body wasn't protected by the metallic scales and my sword cut right through it. The creature let out a horrendous cry. That will teach him a lesson, I thought with satisfaction. He then leapt up and lunged at me from above. If the rocking of the boat had been a disadvantage to me so far, it turned into an advantage now. The creature's lunge capsized the boat towards him and his jaws missed me as I fell. For a brief instant while falling I saw the unprotected underside of the creature's neck close to me, and not bothering about where I was being flung I gave it what in polo would be termed an under the belly shot, the sword slicing upwards. My trusty blade lopped right through his neck, the metal above splitting asunder with a 'prang'. When I splashed into the water, I could hardly believe that I had killed a horrendous sea monster. Talk about mythological heroes! I landed in the water alongside my boat. But in its dying throes, the leviathan whipped his tail and struck the boat. It shattered but did not hurt me as I was hurled like a tennis ball. Fortunately, this achieved what I had been trying to do. I went and landed right next to the craggy shoal. Dazed but feeling the reviving chill of the water, I quickly scrambled to the shore.

But if I thought I had killed the monster, I found I was sadly mistaken. As I hauled myself on to the rocky ledge, I looked back and to my horror saw the creature writhe up, his armoured head on top of his neck and whole again. On the side I saw the head I had decapitated floating in the water. The monster had grown a new head immediately. With a sinking heart I realized that such a creature would be impossible to kill. Without thinking of the pain I was in from being flung, I ran as best I could towards the exit. I was next to the cliff and in the light of the torches in the cave I was surprised to see my fur coat lying on the ground in the gateway. The creature had now clambered on to the strand and the horrible thing could run almost as fast as he could swim. He would soon catch me. Then I saw how my coat had got there. Sru emerged from under it and waved at me. Damn fool, couldn't he find a better time to be friendly.

'Meeru! Meeru! Quickly, get to one side and hide! Cover your eyes!' he shouted.

If I tried to hide, that thing would see me and be upon me in a moment. The imp, keeping himself covered by my fur coat, ran forward and I saw he also had one of those flares. The thought flashed through my mind, 'That's a good idea,' and quickly ducked to one side, hurriedly looking in the other direction. The flare ignited with a blinding flash. For a few moments everything was bathed in a dazzling white light that smarted the eyes, even though it had happened behind me. The sea monster was not too far away, but paralysed by the glare it was forced to stop. I was now looking towards the entrance and I saw the clever imp had hidden himself again by getting under my fur coat. He was right near the niche of the orange demon. Then to my horror I saw movement in the alcove. The flare had wakened the orange demon!

'Meeru! Hide!' Sru shouted, poking his head out from under my fur coat again.

'Hide? Where?' I thought in a panic. The next moment the frightful demon clambered down from the alcove. He stood there for a moment, stretching his arms, the huge axe stiff in his arms as he looked around.

'The fool! What had he done!?' I thought desperately. Now I had the sea monster behind me and this dreadful creature in front.

The demon started striding towards me. I got a whiff, like that of a plethora of stale flowers. It was the odour of the gargantuan from waking after a long sleep. There was no escape. I uttered a wail of despair and flung myself into a declivity behind some rocks nearby to hide myself as best I could. However, the next moment the demon saw the sea monster, and with a blood-curdling snarl he dived, literally flying with its axe towards the monstrous amphibian. He threw great bolts of fire at him, but the monster retracted his neck and curled down so that only his armour was in front and the flaming bursts couldn't harm the metal. Then the demon attacked him with his axe and the monster tried to grab it with his mouth. It was a clash of titans. The ground shook as the two horrendous creatures fought right next to the rocks where I was hiding.

Sru ran back to the entrance and shouted to me, 'Meeru! Meeru! Run! Get out!' But with the monster's tail flailing about and the two ghastly creatures grappling with each other hardly a few yards away, all I could do was cower lower behind the rocks, certain that I was going to die. Then the demon lopped off the head of the monster, but the next instant another grew back. This took the demon by surprise and the amphibian grabbed him in his mouth. The demon squirmed and writhed desperately, using his strength to pry open the monster's jaws to free himself, and with a heave he managed to jump out. At once he grabbed the sea monster from the front with his hands. He lifted the leviathan, five times his size, and flung it. The rocks shattered where he hit. The monster's tail struck the rocks where I was hiding and some of them smashed into bits. Thank heavens I was crouching on the ground, but now I had lost my cover. With lightning swiftness, the demon jumped on the monster's unprotected underside and began to hack it with his axe. The next instant a number of tentacles suddenly shot out of the gash and began to entangle the demon. He desperately chopped away at them and was able to leap off, landing right near where I was crouching on the ground. The wounds on the monster began to heal immediately and he struggled to get up. I heard the demon audibly gasp in exertion, before he brought down a pillar of fire on to the belly of the monster. The horrible leviathan let out a bellowing cry and burst into flames.

'Come on, Meeru!' Sru shouted.

The demon stood looking at the creature burning to cinders. This was going to be my only opportunity. I got up and began to edge towards the exit so as not to attract attention, because the demon was right beside me looking in the other direction. Then he turned around. 'Now I've had it!' I thought, wilting inside with fear. I knew he was too fast. If I ran, he would grab me. I gave him a weak smile and continued to edge away, hoping with all my heart that he wouldn't bother about me. I was now beside my fur coat. I bent down to pick it up. The demon took two strides towards me. I stopped, frozen in fear. The creature was now towering above me. I held my sword to at least try to defend myself. But the next moment the creature bent down, snatched my fur coat away from me and held it up as if admiring it. Apparently he had lost interest in me. Well, of course I regretted forgoing my expensive coat, but obviously I had no option. I quickly edged away and then Sru and I ran up the stairs before that demon ancestor decided to look for more booty. It was just too bad about the coat. How was I ever going to explain this to Ammi?

7

Back to Hashtpur

Now I had made up my mind to go to Hashtpur. As we went up the stone stairs, Sru explained to me what had happened. He told me that the female halfling had died. I couldn't help feeling upset. Then when the halfling had heard I'd gone to the Sea of Shadows, he had followed us down the steps and blown the horn that summoned the sea monster to kill me.

'Why did you come down? Why didn't you take your chance and leave?' I asked him.

'And miss all the fun and excitement? I can leave any time now, but I must say I thoroughly enjoyed myself. I hope you get into more trouble, manusya.'

'No, thank you. For your information, it wasn't fun and I was too busy saving my life to notice anything exciting. All the same, I'm very grateful to you. If you hadn't turned up, I'd be dead. You've saved my life for the second time. But tell me, didn't you realize the flare would wake the orange demon?'

'Of course. The flash is enough to wake the dead. That's why I rushed forward.'

'Then how did you know the creature would prefer to attack the sea monster and not kill me first.'

'Frankly, I didn't. It was a fifty-fifty chance,' Sru said thoughtfully, waving his fingers in a delicate manner to indicate how dicey it had been.

'Well, I'm still alive so I guess it's thanks to you. I can't take any more of this. Anyway, I've got to return to my own world.'

'You're leaving?' he asked, a hint of sadness in his voice.

'Yes, I've found out all I could here. Now I've got to go while I still have my life.'

'Don't go. Stick around. Don't worry, I'll protect you,' he said, becoming emotional.

'That's another thing that frightens me,' I couldn't help commenting, but I felt bad seeing how sad he had become. 'I'm sorry, my small friend, but my quest is taking me in another direction. I have to go back. Why don't you come with me?'

'No, I can't. No dhakana has ever gone to the world of humans. Who knows what monsters dwell in your world.'

Well, he was right about that.

~

When we came to my room, I got another shock. A skull dripping blood was placed on the threshold.

'Good heavens! What is this?' I asked.

'Oh dear! Oh dear! This is a sign, a very bad sign,' Sru told me. 'This is the handiwork of that wizard I stole . . . err . . . took the necklace from,' he continued. 'It's an ancient hex that is supposed to bring death. My grandfather told me all about it. However, you are safe as long as you don't cross that threshold, manusya. So you call the caretaker and send him in to get your luggage. Heh! Heh! Though he's not the target, perhaps the hex will get him,' he said, sniggering, and went and kicked the skull to one side. 'Of course, we can't have him see this. But beware, manusya! This is a very bad sign. It means that creature has vowed vengeance on you. He won't rest till he kills you. He must be angry at you for slaying his mate.'

'It was an accident. She rushed forward on to my sword.'

'But that's not the way the wizard sees it. You've seen the grizzly memento he has left you. Be very careful, manusya,' said Sru, wide-eyed and shaking his head. 'That wizard is determined to kill you. No doubt he'll follow you to your own world and I won't be around to protect you. So wear the amulet at all times, even while you sleep. Don't let it out of your sight.'

Then unable to contain his emotions, he burst into tears, hugged my knees and exclaimed, 'Oh dear!' I bent down to hug him.

'Life is going to be so boring without you. I'm going to miss you,' he said. 'Maybe we'll meet again somehow.'

I also felt emotional leaving him. I had grown quite fond of him and it was extremely doubtful that I'd ever see him again.

The caretaker came to see me. I told him I was leaving and asked him to get my things. I informed him about the hex and the skull lying in the corner. He said he would take care of it. In keeping with the hospitality of the place he packed me some food and gave me a thick woollen coat to compensate for the one I had lost and so I wouldn't freeze on the way back. I also took along some of the magic flares.

Going back was easier. When I came to the tunnels, I ignited one of the flares and the bhasakalas flew out shrieking and squawking. Did I say it was easier? Sorr-rry! The mountainous steps seemed more perilous going down. Sherpa children could probably just skip along on them. I should have been immune to fear after what I had been through. But my life was very precious to me and the precarious danger I was facing on the slopes could end it just as effectively as the others I had faced in Sikkinsala. Several times on my way down I got stuck, frozen in fear and inched along desperately grasping whatever I could to stabilize myself. It took me two days to reach the Dom monastery.

As soon as I took my foot off the last step, my Tibetan coat suddenly disintegrated into ashes and my sword and shield became dull and rusty. After all, they were thousands of years old. I felt bad about my weapons, but it made me realize just how far behind I had left Sikkinsala with its magic and dangers and one nice friend. At last I was safely back in my own world.

~

The monks got very excited when they saw me coming and welcomed me enthusiastically. They all questioned me about Sikkinsala. The bespectacled monk translated everything I said for the others. Then the older one had a scribe write down all I told them of the fabled place.

'What about your quest? Were you successful?' the translator monk asked me after I finished.

I told him I hadn't been able to find out anything about my beloved. 'But at least now I know where the demon who was sent to kill her is and I'm going to confront him and make him tell me what he did with her.'

When he looked doubtful, I quickly told him about the necklace and the magic sword I had and explained the gist of my plan.

He listened to me attentively and translated what I had said to his guru.

The old man looked surprised. He turned to me involuntarily and began to tell me something that I obviously couldn't understand. He realized his mistake soon and related the rest of what he had to say to the bespectacled monk, who then explained to me, 'Young sire, you must be very careful. The demon you seek will be very powerful. Some demons are more powerful than others. Some are kings in the realm of demons. Their ancestors used to be kings in past ages, but after they were defeated they went into hibernation. Some demons are warriors and they are very powerful too. The higher class of demons is raj jinns. Female demons are as powerful as their male counterparts. Apart from having physical powers, many of these jinns are also adept at various kinds of magic. They are taught by venerable demon sorcerers and sorceresses. The older a jinn gets the more powerful he becomes. Below the raj jinns are the aseers. Known to be very nasty, they sometimes enter our world and take possession of some poor person or cause blights. They can suck the life force out of their victims and gain their strength. Below them are the deos – black, fiendish creatures who eat humans. The realm of demons is watched over by the old ones.'

'Yes, I've heard of them. Hishoo told me about them.'

'They are a few old kings from very ancient times. Over the millennia, they became so powerful that their bodies transformed into spirits. They have especially powerful jinns to do their bidding, mightier than other raj jinns. My guru talks of a monstrous scorpion and her brood of demon children, who serve the old ones. No doubt the demon you seek is also a messenger of the old ones. Therefore, even though your necklace will protect you, you should not forget that you are dealing with one of the most dangerous creatures of the demon world.'

Well, at least now I wouldn't have Sru to help me, which all things considered I felt was a good thing. I thanked the monks for their advice. After that they treated me to a lavish meal. As I sat and ate with them, I began to wonder how different it was being back in my own world with fellow humans, even Tibetan monks, and what a precious thing life was.

I had missed the last bus from Nakchu. The monks very kindly told me that I could spend the night in the monastery and leave in the morning. In the evening there was a snowstorm and it was impossible to tell when twilight was over and night-time began. Fortunately, the monks gave me a blanket to keep me warm since I had lost my fur coat. While we sat silently listening to the wind outside, I suddenly noticed that my sword and shield had become shining and new again. I was surprised and pointed this out to my translator monk. At once the elder monk became nervous and said something to the others. My translator told me this could only mean that there was some asura nearby, maybe even watching us through the window. I quickly picked up my sword and shield and told them not to worry. If it came in, I would protect them. They assured me that it was all right as demons sometimes passed by on their way to the portal. They would take care of the situation. Still I couldn't help being surprised and said it must be very difficult for an asura to be out in a snowstorm like this. My translator told me that it must be a demon of air, who were creatures of the cold. He also told me that I had probably not seen all of Sikkinsala as there was an area there where asuras of air were housed. More reassuringly, he informed me that apparently the magic of my sword was still working and it would become active whenever I needed it.

Then all the monks sat on the floor in a circle, closed their eyes and began to hum. The humming seemed to harmonize together and amplified greatly, filling the room. Then I noticed that my sword and shield had become rusty again. So this was the way they drove away demons and it seemed to be effective. Later we all retired for the night. We slept on flat platforms in one room. It was somewhat uncomfortable, but after all I had been through I can't tell you how nice and secure I felt lying with other humans around, and particularly those who knew about and had strange powers to deal with the supranatural.

~

When I landed in Patna, I took a train to the old historical city of Agra for which I had an entry permit since I had intended to call on my cousins who lived there. Shehzad sent a chauffeur and a Mercedes to pick me up from the station in grand style. First the chauffeur took me to the hotel I had booked. I checked in, deposited my luggage and washed up. I decided to leave the amulet behind. Though it would be well hidden under my jacket, I didn't want to take the risk of my cousins spotting it on me. The chauffeur took me to the princelings' house. It was a newly built, sprawling mansion. I was informed that it was designed by a famous architect. It was surrounded by a high wall, the state's emblem was emblazoned on the gate and armed guards stood watch, as if the princes were still of consequence. Shehzad welcomed me warmly at the porch. Lucky guy, he was already married. He introduced me to his family. His wife was a knockout. Regardless of whatever she had heard about me, she was very courteous and I was served sumptuous tea, with pastries, patties, gulab jamuns, the works. Anyway, I was fond of Shehzad; he had always been the nicer of the two. He told me Shehbaz was out of town. Probably avoiding me, I thought. I commiserated about the death of his mother.

You're probably wondering about all the hypocrisy, what with the bad blood and legal case between us and everything else. Well, being brought up amid palace intrigues one learns to retain one's genuine feelings for another and, despite who is conspiring against whom, the code of etiquette and show of affection must always be observed unless one is going to have the person arrested or ousted the next minute.

'Yes, it was awful. The despicable brutes decapitated her,' he said bitterly.

Of course, he couldn't dream of the real reason.

'You know, the villains didn't rob anything. It was almost as if the family curse got her. Who knows, maybe these things go awry now and then. We'd hoped with the realm gone the curse would be lifted as well. You know, somebody stole the amulet on the night when Koyel bhan was killed.'

'Really? I wondered where it was,' I said nervously, glad that I had left the amulet in the hotel.

'By the way, it was nice of Phupi Sobia to make that gesture of recognizing Ammi's right over Zeenat Mahal before her death, even if it was only a formality. But I'm glad that at least you people have a proper place to stay.'

'Thank you, Shehzad. Please forgive and forget any differences between us,' I said sincerely.

'Don't talk nonsense,' he replied flippantly, and I realized why I liked him. That, and the eclairs he offered me.

Then he looked at me with narrowed eyes. 'I notice you've come from Patna. What did you go there for?'

'Actually, I had to go to Tibet.'

'Tibet? I hope you're not involved in an international intrigue or something.'

'No, I went on a very personal matter.'

'Personal matter? In Tibet?'

He kept questioning me keenly and I realized I had

to tell him something convincing, especially because I needed his help.

'Please don't tell anybody; the matter is still not finalized. You see, Uncle Shamsheer suggested a rishta for me. She's the daughter of an important lama in Tibet.' This was one of my best ones yet!

'Really, what's her name?'

'In Tibet they don't divulge the names of their daughters. They're very conservative, especially in religious families. Her father is the lama of an important monastery in Lhasa,' I explained, and gave him the name of the lama I had met.

'I thought lamas never married,' he said querulously. Oops! I had forgotten that, but his general knowledge was as bad as mine and he seemed to swallow my ridiculous story. 'Well, that's good news. Imagine, you're getting a Tibetan wife.'

'Inshallah! By the way, I need a little help from you.'

'Certainly, Mehran bhai.'

'I need an entry permit for Hashtpur. I have to go to the old palace.'

He looked doubtful. I understood his hesitation. Shehbaz would get very angry if he found out Shehzad had helped me in any way.

'What do you want to go there for? There's nothing there. The palace has fallen to ruins. They even say it's haunted. The town is practically deserted. Sarmpur, the old market town, is now the main place in that area.'

'Please, I must go. It's important.'

'What's so important? If you want to go for sentimental reasons, I would advise you not to. You'll only get upset when you see the state of our old palace. Vandals haven't left a single piece of marble or tile work.'

'No, it's not for sentimental reasons. I had promised Badi Baaji I'd bring some soil of our homeland for her. She wants to put it on her grave. I have to keep my promise.' I was certainly outdoing myself here.

'Oh, for heaven's sake!' Shehzad said.

'No, it's important. I promised I would do this for her,' I told him with a sincere, beatific expression on my face.

'Oh, all right. I can send someone over there to get that for you. He'll be back by tomorrow evening,' he said.

'No, that won't do. Badi Baaji says I have to collect it myself. Please, Shehzad, I must keep my promise to her,' I said, trying to look even more sincere, to convince him I was the sort of person who kept his word – difficult, ver-ry difficult. By the way, in case you're wondering, I didn't pay Fakhr for his door.

'Well, I suppose it can be arranged,' he said after a moment's thought. 'Do you remember Diwan Vankadram? His son is in the interior ministry. I'm sure old Vankadji will remember you and help you. I'll give you his number and you can contact him yourself. He lives in Delhi. Please don't tell him I gave you his number.'

'Thank you, Shehzad.'

'You better watch out for snakes. They say the old ruins are crawling with them.'

~

It wasn't snakes I had to watch out for. When I got back to my hotel room, I found the lock burnt off and the place ransacked.

The amulet was gone! I was ruined. To be outdone in this manner after everything I had suffered! I wished I had heeded Sru's advice. I had planned on going to Rajwaran and searching for Dajaar Galakara. My amulet would have protected me from him and I would have overpowered him with my weapons. No doubt after ten years he would have picked up Hindi. I would have forced him to tell me what he did with Koyel. For all I knew he might be holding her captive in the old ruins. Who knows the caprices of demons. But now my protection was lost and the plan seemed dicey.

However, that wasn't going to deter me. At least I had my magic sword and shield. The shield would protect me from fireballs and I had proven myself as good as a ninja with my trusty blade. On the other hand, maybe this Dajaar fellow would prove reasonable. It was only information I wanted and if he didn't have any ulterior motive, he might give it to me. Apparently, demons weren't necessarily hostile. Hishoo was a dreadful demon as well but he proved very friendly and helpful. Well, we would see what we would see.

But what did scare me was that now the halfling had the amulet and he was hell-bent on killing me. He could come around any time at night, while I slept, and murder me. I complained to the management about my room being broken into. I didn't tell them what had been stolen in case news of the amulet got back to my cousins. Then I went and checked into another hotel, being careful to ensure I wasn't being followed like a secret agent. Later I telephoned Diwan Vankadram, and he was very helpful. I collected my entry permit from the consulate after two days, again using secret agent tactics.

8

Reaching the Horizon

I took a bus to go to Hashtpur because my budget was running low. A packed bus was also a safer option in case the halfling was following me secretly. I felt a bit self-conscious roughing it in this cheap style in my homeland, but it was unlikely the other rustic passengers would recognize their erstwhile shahzada.

As I leaned my head against the rattling windowpane and looked out at the familiar landscape, I realized just how much of a desert my homeland was – endless sand dunes and bushes interspersed with small, sparse trees. Occasionally the dunes intruded on to the road, fortunately not enough to block the bus. Every few miles the greenery would increase and there would be tracts of ploughed fields, then gradually the sand dunes would take over again. Soon we came to the river, the lifeline of my uncle's realm. When I lived here there had only been a boat bridge across it, but now I found the government had built a proper bridge, albeit only a modest, narrow structure, but I suppose that was all my uncle's kingdom was worth in the eyes of the government. It was so far out in the desert and connected by inadequate lines of communication that the government had left the area more or less undeveloped. In my uncle's time there had been a railway line from Bhatinder that the Raj had built and maintained for political reasons. I remember that all the carriages were emblazoned with our royal crest and people were always coming and going. Hashtpur had been a bustling metropolis then, but now it had lost its importance. The line had proved unfeasible for the railways and they had allowed it to become almost derelict.

Then the landscape became completely barren with a vast, dramatic expanse of bare sand dunes stretching away with rocky mesas in the distance. It evoked a feeling of nostalgia in me and a sort of longing that beauty lay somewhere far away, beyond the horizon. I began to feel that Koyel was somewhere there and I was drawing closer to her. In fact, I was getting good vibes. But the problem with this long, impossible search that I had embarked on and so far faced nothing but repeated disappointments was that sometimes my mind started manufacturing vibes. So I tried to quell these lest I get disillusioned again.

Sarmpur had certainly expanded since I last saw it. I could hardly recognize it. There was no respectable hotel in town and Vankadramji had graciously booked me in a government rest house on the outskirts. After settling in, I bought a fairly good horse since I had heard that the road to Rajwaran was now no longer motorable, besides there was no place to rent a car or hire a taxi in Sarmpur. I quickly set off for my destination. I wanted to reach the old palace as soon as possible so that I could spend more time searching in daylight. I certainly didn't want to confront Dajaar at night. Now I was in more familiar territory and on the way the sights awakened old memories. I passed Zamurrad Shah's old haveli. It was situated behind a high mud wall on the main road and I could see the tops of the trees of his orchard behind the haveli. Poor chap had passed away but his wife and two sons still lived there. I remembered them very well, Changez and Tabrez; as children we used to play together and had a lot of fun. It seemed reassuring that there were still friendly faces here and my childhood home hadn't altered completely. I intended to visit them on my way back and had phoned them that I was coming. They were overjoyed and insisted I stay with them. I looked forward to meeting them once again.

Finally, around two o'clock, I reached Rajwaran. Indeed, it was a shock to see the once-magnificent palace. But it wasn't as bad as Shehzad had described. One half and the front of the building had collapsed, leaving the inside of the great hall right up to the second floor exposed to view like a dilapidated doll's house. The structure looked impossibly surreal and asymmetrical. Everything was in various stages of ruination with crumbling remnants of arches standing incongruously. Rubble and piles of blocks were strewn all around and there were upright open frames of doors leading nowhere. Grass and bushes had grown in nooks and between the rubble, and piles of sand had built up against the debris as nature slowly reclaimed the ruins. But birds were singing and chirping in the winter sunshine, and when I looked up I saw part of Koyel's jharokha with a few panes of coloured glass still standing. I interpreted this as a good omen. But then I saw a brightly coloured snake slither away behind some blocks and I realized this wasn't going to be easy.

Now that I saw the place, I realized what a daunting task it was. The area was huge, and I knew there was a secret chamber here somewhere. It had been built for the royal family to hide in if enemies took over the fort. Unfortunately, I didn't know its location; I only remembered Shehzad once telling me in the library that there was a secret room somewhere there. I hoped that with the place fallen to ruin, the entrance to the chamber had been uncovered. Otherwise I could use my sword on the walls – or rather what remained of them – of the library and if it became new and shiny then I would know that the demon was lurking somewhere behind them.

Later I found out why the palace had collapsed. Shortly after Partition, the wadi nearby had flooded twice since there was nobody to look after the banks. The water had flowed up to the fortress and nothing was done to drain it or repair the damage. It had softened the foundations, and eventually the fortress had collapsed. The outer palisade at the back had also fallen, revealing the vast, trackless desert beyond it, and the ruins of a derelict sarai were about two furlongs away. It looked like a stage set opening on an impossibly extensive and desolate expanse.

I spent the remaining daylight hours searching the broken-down palace. I had forgotten the size of the place and it was a good walk just from the ruined stables to the front fountain. Scrambling over piles of rubble was difficult, and there was also the danger of snakes. My weapons would be useful in guiding me; they would warn me if the demon was near, but they remained rusty all the while. The possibility that I might not even be able to find Dajaar worried me more than what I'd do when I found him.

After several fruitless hours of wandering through bare rooms, when the shadows began to lengthen and evening fell, I got on my horse and headed back, feeling disappointed. I was so preoccupied with my feelings I wasn't thinking of what to expect when I'd reach Zamurrad's haveli, though I was going to meet my childhood friends. Down the road I found a car waiting for me. Apparently they had sent their chauffeur with their car as far along the road that the vehicle could travel to drive me back to their haveli.

At the haveli, they greeted me like a long-lost relative. Though life has many closed chapters, some people do care for you in absentia and reciprocal feelings lie latent in one's own heart. We hugged each other as if to banish twelve years and at once a flood of memories rushed back to me. I remembered Changez's sense of humour. He was always ready to laugh and make you laugh. He'd make a joke about anything: 'You've been to the old palace? They've redone the place, you might have noticed. It's certainly nice and airy, isn't it?'

'Well, the place is definitely done for,' I retorted.

'You shouldn't go there. It's supposed to be haunted,' said Tabrez.

'It must be haunted by the spirit of Kotwal Sanga!' said Changez, laughing, and I went into splits at the memory of our old standing joke.

One day, when we were around eleven years old, we were playing in the back portico of the palace and came across the nawab standing there talking to Kotwal Sanga, one of the more impressive officers of the guard. My uncle was saying something to him and as the tall man with huge moustaches stood listening, suddenly his countenance changed. He raised his face, his expression became set and serious and his moustache bristled. We wondered what was happening to him. Maybe it was because of something the nawab had said. He appeared to be straining. The next moment his body stiffened, and we found out what was wrong. He had been trying to hold back wind in his stomach and finally it exploded with a ripping, bass sound that his horse would have been proud of. We were naughty children and of course we never got over that martial fart.

'The spirits he unleashed that day must still be around.' I laughed.

'Maybe that's what weakened the foundation,' Changez sputtered, beside himself guffawing.

'You shouldn't joke about such things. It really is haunted,' said Tabrez.

Their mother, Safina begum, came out and we quickly shut up.

Later as the chill night set in – the desert can be very cold at night-time – we sat in front of the fire and had a lot to talk about. There was no electricity since the small powerhouse of the old capital of the estate had finally packed up several years ago, and the government hadn't yet got around to bringing electricity to this far-flung semi-desert region, thus the sombre, bare haveli was lit only by lanterns, but we were least bothered and were enjoying ourselves, laughing at just about anything and everything. The hazards and travails of my mission seemed far away and forgotten. Safina begum sat watching our raucous mirth patiently, till finally she asked, 'Why are you here, beta?'

'You'd never believe me if I told you,' I replied seriously.

'We never believed anything you said in any case,' remarked Changez.

'Quiet, beta, can't you see he's serious?' she chided.

'Ammi, Mehran's an inveterate liar.'

'Not inveterate, brilliant,' I corrected.

'See,' said Tabrez, 'he's just as bad as Channu bhai,' remarked Tabrez.

I told them of my dream and the purpose of my visit. I didn't tell them of my interlude in Sikkinsala; that was too fantastic. Nor did I tell them about the taweez, for obvious reasons. But I told them about the halfling and Hishoo, and covered up by saying that Hishoo had told me I would find Dajaar in the ruins and I should ask him what had happened. I also told them that Hishoo had provided me the magic sword and shield. I even gave them a bit of my bark so they could check for demons themselves.

'It sounds fantastic,' Tabrez said in awe.

'Oh, so that's what those rusty old weapons on your horse are. I hope the demon hasn't ripped you off. You didn't pay him anything, did you?' Changez, of course.

'No! No! They really work. They're magic and they become new and shiny when a demon is near. They protected me from Shamoon's fireballs. I fought him off with the sword (I didn't have the heart to tell them about the halfling's mate). They will protect me from Dajaar. Bullets don't affect jinns.'

'He's serious,' commented Tabrez.

'Well, if he's telling the truth, it's serious, and if he's not, it's more serious,' remarked Changez.

'Please, Channu beta, this is an important matter for Shahzada Mehran. He's come all the way from Lahore for this,' Safina begum said, mildly admonishing him, rightfully so in my opinion.

'We know demons exist, though they seldom manifest themselves in this world. Most people don't believe in them, but we have had a sad experience with them,' she continued. 'Somehow Shahzada Mehran has got involved with them and no doubt he has seen some strange things. Whatever the wisdom in what he is doing, it's his wish. His father loved going into the jungle and hunting fierce animals in his time. However, what you are up to, beta, seems very dangerous. Does Rani Sobia know what you are doing?' Safina begum asked.

'No, she'll worry needlessly. Please don't tell her, at least not just yet.'

'But beta, what if something happens to you? Besides, don't you think we'll worry about you too?'

'Please, Maasiji, I've got to do this. I will never be at peace again if I don't find out what happened to Koyel that night and bring her back,' I said, becoming emotional involuntarily.

'You really believe she's alive after what happened and after all these years?'

'I know it. My vision told me so. I've got to find out what really happened that night.'

'Well, I don't know what to say about that, but if this quest is so important to you, why don't you do it the sensible way, the safe way? Hire an amil who knows about such things and let him go out there for you and find out.'

'No! Don't worry, I can take care of myself. I know these weapons don't look like much but you should see them when a jinn comes close. They really are magic and you have no idea what they are capable of. Only a very powerful demon can stand up to me when I have these in my hand,' I said to reassure her, but that only seemed to worry her more. I continued earnestly, 'Besides, I have to do this myself. You see, an amil will only use his traditional knowledge and everybody I've met tells me the same story, that Koyel is dead. The amil will probably arrive at the same conclusion, because that's what the evidence indicates. But I know she's alive. I have to do it myself in order to go a little deeper, to find clues others would miss and learn the truth for myself. So please don't tell Ammi I'm here, at least not just yet, for the sake of my family,' I pleaded.

She looked doubtful, but I could tell that I had gotten my message across, and much against her better judgement she wouldn't stop me from what I was doing.

If I had been anybody else she would have immediately put her foot down, so I guess being ex-royalty was still worth something.

'We'll come and help you,' said Tabrez.

'No, it's dangerous. I'm searching for a demon. It's not a game. You won't be able to defend yourselves against him. At least I have my sword and shield.'

My friends still didn't quite know what to make of my story and it took a lot of convincing for them to let me continue searching the ruins alone.

'Okay, but if you ever need help, we're there for you,' Tabrez assured me.

After that we went for dinner, which had its own hazards.

'Where should I sit?' I asked.

'On your bottom, of course. That's where normal people sit,' Changez replied.

'Oh nuts! I should have known better than to ask you a simple question.'

'Simple people ask simple questions,' he said, nodding sagaciously, before adding, 'Good heavens! Have you thought what impression the demons must have of the human race having you as an example?'

'Better than what they would have if they had met you. It's lucky you didn't come across them,' I retorted promptly, and then added, 'Perhaps it would have been better if you had.'

The servant brought in dinner, served in the lavish

style as it was in the palace in the old days with each item under a silver dish cover.

'Ah ha!' said Changez, uncovering a round dish cover for me. 'Mehran, prepare to meet your dome.'

Fortunately, their mother entered and he had to behave himself, except when during the course of the meal I made the mistake of asking him, 'Changez, can you pass me a roti, please?'

'Of course. I'll pass it in the morning. That's usually when I pass what I've eaten.'

'Changez!' Safina begum exclaimed, shocked.

The meal was delicious. I had forgotten how tasty the meals in outlying farms could be, with homegrown wheat and vegetables cooked in desi ghee on a log fire. It was getting late and the night outside was chilly and dark. I begged leave.

'You can't go,' said Changez.

'Yes, I can,' I replied.

'No, you have to stay with us. We've prepared a room for you. And the roads are dangerous at night. There have been a number of deaths.'

'Dacoits?' I asked.

'Worse. Thuggees. There's a gang of them that has been operating here for some time. We'll send for your luggage in the morning.'

~

For three days I continued my one-sided game of hide-and-seek in the ruins to no avail. My sword and shield remained rusty. I was getting more and more frustrated and began to wonder if the sequencer was right. Or maybe the demon had left. By now I had searched almost every nook and corner of the place. I hadn't been able to discover the secret chamber yet. That was my only hope now.

On the afternoon of the third day, a strange thing happened. The sun was so bright that the glare impaired rather than improved my vision and a dusty wind was blowing. Suddenly I heard the scrunch of some gravel behind me. I quickly looked in the direction of the sound. There was a big pile of dust-covered debris behind me. My eyes went to the top of the mound and I had to squinch my eyes to see in the bright sunlight and all the dust blowing about. For a fleeting second I thought I saw a figure duck out of sight on top of the mound, or it might have been a wave of dust. I checked my sword; it was still rusty. I scrambled up the mound so that if it had been someone or something I would be able to see them running away. However, when I got to the top there was nothing. The place was empty and utterly silent, except for the whistling sound of the wind. Then I realized I had not heard any birds chirping. On previous days there had always been some bird calls. Something must have scared them off. Was I being watched? It couldn't have been a demon since my sword was rusty, or perhaps it hadn't come close enough to affect my weapons. But something had frightened the birds away, or maybe they were affected by the strong wind? I couldn't be certain. I looked around uneasily. I searched for footprints. There were none but the wind could have blown them away.

I kept my sword ready. That afternoon I combed the ruins of the servant quarters. They were still standing. Several times I thought I heard some sound but it could have been the wind blowing rubble. At times I distinctly felt an eerie sensation, as if someone was watching me, though such feelings can be deceptive. If it was a demon it could attack me any time, however, so far my sword had remained unchanged. The thought occurred to me that perhaps it wasn't anything supernatural at all. I recalled the warning Changez had given me of thuggees. Since then I had started carrying my two-two pistol with me. But the idea of being spied upon by a gang of sworn killers still made me nervous. I kept a lookout for footprints, but didn't come across any. The place was crawling with snakes and all enclosed spaces had traces of their squiggly trails in the dust.

As I left the line of rooms and clambered up a mound of debris, something made me look back. I thought I glimpsed a figure slip away into the shadows of one of the rooms. At once I turned around and dashed back, my sword ready. The room was empty. I looked around at the bare walls but could see no one; only my constant companion, the wind outside, blew wisps of dust in through the non-existent door, but I could have sworn someone had been there a moment ago. I got a few whiffs of a lingering aroma in the air, and then I noticed my sword was shining. Yes, something was watching me all right; something emotionally affected by my presence, and that had made its body odour increase. I quickly looked at the dusty ground for footprints. There were none, except for the marks of slithering snakes.

~

Another futile day was over, with the sun, a huge red ball, descending into the dusty haze of the horizon. I couldn't help wondering how whoever it was could have disappeared. While searching the ruins I always kept myself primed by eating the bark to see any invisible demons or creatures, so if there had been anything watching me I would have spotted it. But I could see nothing. However, I was certain there was somebody or something. What could it be? Why was it watching me? Was it friendly or malevolent? And most importantly, why was it emotionally affected by my presence? Yes, I was convinced what I sensed was correct. The sensation was too strong to deny. The fact is that what we call instinct or intuition is basically just a process of logic and reading from experiences that we have had, but they follow an abstract pattern based on forgotten or half-sensed observations, so we arrive at an intuitive conclusion without knowing why. I told you that I have a strong sense of smell. Well, the odour was corporeal. It had emanated from flesh and blood and it had left its imprint in the air of the room. Yes, spectres and ghosts can disappear, but they aren't made of flesh and blood. The slight trace of odour I got at once evoked an image of a form standing there watching me and being affected by some deep emotions, not necessarily nice emotions. What was I to it, or it to me? Was I trespassing? Somehow in the midst of all this the aura awakened memories of Koyel. Whatever it was, I instinctively felt it could tell me about my dearest childhood companion. But now sensing that this unseen person or whatever it was was watching me made my task more difficult. I would have to be doubly alert and careful as I searched the ruins.

Tabrez and Changez's mother asked me how my search was progressing. I unburdened all my disappointment, frustration and even my fears on her. 'How can I go on?' I almost started crying. She looked sympathetic and then said, 'Perhaps I can help you. Shahji taught me a few things about divination. Maybe the cards can give us a clue about what you are seeking.'

She brought a lamp and placed it on the table. Then she took out an old pack of Mongolian tarot cards and sat down.

'I better tell you that the cards do not answer direct questions. They only give signs and it is up to us to interpret them.'

She then told me to close my eyes and concentrate on what I wanted to know and lay the cards out in a certain way. Then one by one she flipped the cards.

'Ah! We come to the night of the red moon. The card of the eclipse of the moon, since there's no card for a red moon. Sure enough, here's the demon wearing a crown of fire. Oh dear!' she said quietly.

'What? What is it? Is it something about Koyel?'

'Please don't be upset, beta. I see that a jinn killed Koyel. See, he's holding a lamb in his hand, the symbol of innocence; he has just killed a lamb.'

'No, it can't be! Another creature of darkness also told me the demon killed a girl that night. But he didn't say who it was. Perhaps it was someone else. I've seen my cousin alive, and as you saw on that night, she was spirited away; her head was not decapitated like the other victims of the curse! Your card does not specify it was the shahzadi,' I said desperately.

'My dear, these divinations don't specify names, they just give indications about what happened or is going to happen. I'm sorry but it's clear that the demon killed a young girl that night and she was the person he had come to kill. The rest of us were unharmed. Koyel was the only one anything happened to. I think it will be better for you if you accept the possibility that your cousin is dead.'

I looked at the colourful card awhile. It was only a picture; it wasn't going to change and I wasn't able to decipher any other hidden message.

'Let's continue,' I said sadly.

Suddenly my aunt looked surprised.

'This is very strange,' she muttered.

'What is?' I asked anxiously.

'I see another mysterious figure present that night. See, this card shows the raja's entourage, and the next card shows another jinn.'

'Good heavens! You're right.'

'Apparently there were two jinns present that night. See, he is wearing a crown of ice, therefore he's a jinn of air.'

My memory was awakened. I remembered that on that night I had smelt two distinct and different fragrances, like demons have, and one was reminiscent of fresh air.

'Yes, you're correct. Why did they come?' I asked.

'It's clear that they both came for Koyel.'

'But what does this mean?' I said, my stomach twisting at the realization that my theory about the manner of death had suddenly found another possibility.

'Who can say. It could be that the demon of air is immune to the taweez,' my aunt remarked. 'Wait! There's more,' she said.

'What is it?'

'I can't make out. A stranger, the man with the mask – I can't tell if he's human or supernatural – is also present.'

'I know who that must be. He's the amil exorcist who was present that night. I told you, he's actually a halfling and has been following me around.'

'There's a black bird present in his card and in the card of the demon of fire, which means there's some link between him and the demon you seek.'

Well, one thing was certain: there had been more going on that night than any of us had imagined.

'On the other hand, there's no link between the two demons. That's understandable because demons of fire and demons of air hate each other.'

'Perhaps . . .' I said, another thought occurring to me. 'Perhaps the second demon is friendly. After all, I have known friendly jinns.'

'I assure you, this demon is evil. The cards have shown him as black, which is a sign it is evil. Jinns of air can be more dangerous than those of fire.'

Suddenly my aunt turned very pale.

'Oh dear!' she gasped.

'What is it?' I asked.

'The star of blood. Look . . . look down here. The stone floor and chairs are drenched in blood,' she said, horrified.

~

The next morning, the fourth day, I set off feeling quite discouraged. It seemed hopeless to be pottering around those old ruins. Before I left the house, my hostess warned me to be careful. She gave me a charmed bracelet to wear for protection. It was made of silver, which is reputed to have powers against the supernatural. It was of a crude design and about four inches wide, like bracelets worn by barbarian warriors.

The only hope I had was from the secret chamber. With thoughts about the thuggees and the feeling of being watched, I deliberately tied my horse in a hidden nook inside the ruined outer wall of the palace, after making sure I hadn't been followed and nobody had seen me.

Fortunately, the wind wasn't too strong. However, there were still no birds chirping. I looked at the vista of the ruins and in the glaring sunlight indeed it looked haunted, and not just by the demon I was searching for. Who knows what secrets lay hidden in this debris.

As I completed the fairly long walk to what was left of the palace, I suddenly heard a woman singing in the distance. The wind carried the sound in the air, sometimes rising so I could hear the notes fairly distinctly; sometimes falling and becoming inaudible, just leaving a melodious aura over the ruins. Whoever it was had an enchanting voice that didn't need instruments to accompany it. The song imbued the derelict place with a sense of hidden loveliness, of magic casements opening on to a secluded lush garden with pavilions, and an air of ages past. I tried to see where the song was coming from. Surely someone with such a lovely voice must herself be as beautiful to behold. And then, near a broken arch in the distance, I saw a female figure dressed in blue. It was only a fraction of a second before she slipped away into the half-standing rooms, but I definitely saw someone. I hurriedly went in that direction. Sure enough, the sound of the singing got more distinct in the broken line of arches of the main hall. It was a very sad tune that wrenched the heart, but felt strange. It had an undulating lilt unlike any genre of music I had heard before, and it evoked an alien, almost eerie feeling.

I can guess what you're thinking. No, it wasn't Koyel. I knew that. Though I'm not much for the arts, I do have an ear for music and this air hypnotized me. I followed the trail of the music.

Now it seemed to come from somewhere deeper, where it began to echo, and after a little while all that remained were melodic echoes still reverberating in my mind. I looked around and found I was in the ruins of the library. It was odd that the sound seemed to echo, as if it was coming from some large chamber. And then it hit me. Of course, this was the library, and whoever was singing must have gone into the secret chamber. I quickly looked around. The walls that hadn't fallen exposed the entirety of the room, so the secret entrance couldn't be there. I tapped the hilt of my sword on the floor and sure enough, one spot gave out a hollow sound.

I looked around to see if I could find something like a metal bar to pry open the large slab of stone. Nothing. Scavengers had taken away every loose bit of metal. I was loath to use my sword, lest the levering bend the thin metal. However, since I couldn't find anything else, I tentatively tried my blade. It easily fitted into the slits outlining the slab. I applied a little weight. The sword was magical and didn't bend at all. Slowly it began to nudge the slab open. I tried to do this from all sides and just as I began to think it was going to be a very difficult task, I heard a click and the slab flicked up a bit on one side. My efforts must have triggered the opening mechanism. Feeling very excited, I lifted the slab up and underneath I saw broad stone steps going down.

It got darker and darker as I descended the stairs. I arrived at a chamber fairly deep underground. The only light here was from the open slab above me. I wished I had thought of bringing a light. No sir, I wasn't going to confront Dajaar in the dark. Fortunately, beside the entrance of the chamber where the steps ended, I found packets of candles and matches stocked conveniently on a shelf. No doubt they were there for whoever had business in the secret chamber and were covered with dust from long disuse. I lit a candle and peered into the darkness. It was a large tunnel-like room and the candle hardly illuminated the portion where I was standing. The bare brick walls and roof stretched into impenetrable blackness ahead. Surprisingly, the place was full of furniture and decorative items carefully stored and covered with sheets. Someone, at some point of time, must have shifted most of the furniture of the palace down here for safekeeping, probably to prevent the government from taking possession of it. There were many rows of sofas, shelves holding porcelain ornaments, chairs and tables, and numerous statues. Most of them were covered with white sheets. The expensive carpets were rolled in polythene and lined the sides.

'Shehzad might not know about this,' I thought. 'I better tell him ... if I come out of here alive.' I checked my sword. It was still rusty.

The place smelt dank and musty. I went forward cautiously, keeping my scimitar ready, my senses alert and my eyes trying to pierce the Stygian shadows ahead. I kept lighting a candle every ten yards or so and placing them on the small tables or other items of furniture that I uncovered. It was a very long chamber. My steps echoed as I went on. I could see the elaborate chandeliers hanging from the ceiling, unlighted and with no electrical connection, the glass beads glittering in the slight gleam of the candles. One of those would certainly have given me plenty of light. I could recognize most of the items under the sheets – the sofa set from my mother's suite, the two tall candelabras made of Persian glass, the nawab's glass throne, and also the statues from the hall and the garden. I had no idea there were so many; I couldn't recognize some of them: one was particularly tall, standing further away at the edge of the darkness. Covered with sheets and surrounded by silence, everything seemed sinister. I couldn't help thinking that the demon could very well be hiding under one of those sheets. I thought of a joke to tell Changez later. 'Like people say "my trusty blade", I could say "my rusty blade".' I looked at it and saw it was gleaming.

I was immediately on my guard, looking around. The light of the line of candles was very scanty and there were shadows all around and darkness twenty paces in front. I looked towards the tall statue. It wasn't there. The sheet was lying on the ground.

I heard a slight rushing noise and saw a shadow dash at high speed behind some sideboards. I edged cautiously in that direction. I had difficulty finding my voice – my mouth was so dry – but I half whispered, half uttered, 'Dajaar, is that you? I am not your enemy. I just want to ask you something.'

A deep, ominous growl echoed in the long chamber, and I heard another rushing sound. I quickly wheeled around in that direction. How could I watch all sides at the same time? Now I was really scared. But this was what I had come to do.

'Dajaar, speak to me, please,' I said again.

Another bestial growl, much louder. Fear gripped me and the echo of the sound seemed to fill my mind. Then, almost as if from inside my head, I heard a bellowing voice say, 'I am not Dajaar.'

'Please, even if you are not Dajaar, I must speak to you. Can you tell me about Koyel, our princess who disappeared twelve years ago on the night of the red moon?' I almost shouted into the shadows.

An echo seemed to die away in my head, hardly audible. Suddenly an angry resonance assailed my mind. 'You have interfered where you should not have. You must die!'

A chill ran down my spine. In a flash I realized that this must be the demon of air. Yes, I even got the slight whiff of a fragrance. They say odours linger longer in the mind than memories, and I recognized the aroma immediately as the second one I had smelt years ago. I quickly ducked to one side. I certainly couldn't defend myself like this. I took cover behind an uncovered glass cabinet and crept to the edge with my sword and shield, ready to look into the rest of the chamber. But instead, right behind me, reflected in the dark glass and lit waveringly by a candle, I saw a face, a hideous face. It was only a momentary glimpse but heightened for a second by the flare of the candle. The face was round, white and gleaming smooth, like porcelain with incredibly evil, slanting slits for eyes, and in place of a nose an angular crease came down the glossy planate features, leading not to nostrils but a sort of beak, like a Maori war mask, with two open, snarling circles on either side revealing slavering black jowls, the inside of its mouth bright red, with brutish, curved fangs. The terrifying sight made my blood run cold. In a panic I turned around and tried to attack the figure with my sword, but it had disappeared. Desperate and trembling with fear, I looked this way and that to figure out where it could have come from. Suddenly there was a hum, like that of a superfast turbine, and the next moment I felt a chill grip me. I heard a loud crack from the outer corner of the shelf and a dozen crevices appeared on it, the glass shattering almost explosively. It happened in a split second. I felt like I was freezing but the next instant my shield and sword burst into flames, heating up the place.

I realized that the sneaky demon must have caused some sort of deadly cryogenic blast; clearly this one was only a slanting blow that had knocked out the glass shelf, and my magical weapons had miraculously flamed up and prevented the body-numbing chill from harming me. I couldn't help wonder why the demon didn't blast me when he was right behind me earlier. Even now he had only thrown a slanting ray that hit the shelf, which meant that as soon as he got to a clear angle he would fire straight at where I was standing. I quickly ran from that death trap to the back of the shelf, and not a moment too soon because what happened next was like something out of a sci-fi film where ray guns devastate an area completely; though instead of luminescent beams and incendiary blasts there were brief flashes that I hardly saw, a rush of air streaking forward with slight, random darting filaments of ice coalescing in the air, and when the beam struck there were resounding metallic twangs and loud crackling noises. Cold wave coronas flashed one after the other and shrapnel of frozen crystals shattered all around with a freezing mist billowing up. The swirling, scintillating mist obliterated the space where I had been standing until it was only a mass of frozen shapes.

I could feel the bitter chill that emanated from that place as I crept away using the cover of a line of sofas, my weapons wisely not flaming and giving away my position. I thanked my lucky stars that I left that spot when I did and I was now trying to head back to the entrance. I had to get out. It was stupid to try to fight this demon. Only once I had put some more shelves between him and me did I dare raise my head to look around. A bronze statue of a Turkish warrior with sword drawn stood on a pedestal near me. Again I heard that short, high-speed hum and then a loud clang. At once the statue in front of me reduced to half its size, became highly glazed and the next moment shattered into a million pieces. I felt a freezing blast and saw the jet stream of icy mist from the cryogenic bolt when it hit the statue. My faithful shield lit up with a warm, fiery glow. I knew I was next. I quickly lifted my shield, but even as I did it seemed to raise itself further to cover my face, and the very next second the frigid bolt hit it with the impact of a flying cricket ball. There was a loud hiss, followed by steam, and a cascade of water poured out from where the icy blast had come in contact with the red-hot shield. Wow! Bless Shaminitsu, his magical shield not only provided thermal safety but also moved itself to protect the defender from wherever the blasts may hit.

I crouched low and scuttled away, protecting myself with the mass of furniture. The entrance was still far away. How was I going to get out of this mess? I moved my shield on to my back in case any bolts came from behind. I saw some rapid movement near the shelves behind me. I heard an ominous snarl and could see a shadow elongate in the candlelight. Now that thing could overtake me any moment and attack me from any side, and my shield might not be able to protect me. There was only one thing to do. Leaving behind the cover provided by the furniture, I ran to the side of the tunnel so that nothing could attack me from the back at least. All my senses alert and holding my shield up, I edged forward with my back against the damp wall.

From down the dark hall came a dreadful, bestial growl that echoed and became louder. Something flew through the air and landed to my right. I could see a dark shadow moving in the lee of a pile of crates. I kept edging away gingerly, moving as quickly as possible.

And then the candles began extinguishing one by one, starting with the one nearest to the entrance.

'Oh no!' I screamed and started running before darkness overtook me. Just as the last candle went out, I saw some rubble on the ground and a black crevice in the wall. A portion of the tunnel had caved in at that spot. In the gathering darkness I saw the light from the other side. I quickly entered the slight cavity that had been created. Some underground water seemed to have washed away a deposit of mud lining the tunnel and the ground above had fallen into the fissure that had been created. There was a pile of rubble in front and on top was a small aperture, with roots hanging all around. I could see daylight, which almost seemed surprising after the permanent night of the secret chamber. I put the sword back in its sheath and hitched the shield on my back to quickly scramble up the rubble before that frightening creature came after me. Once on top of the pile, I had to leap to grab hold of some roots. It was a risky move in case I didn't jump high enough, missed the roots or if the roots didn't hold. I'd tumble back down the six-foot pile and who knows when that creature would burst into this place, but I was so afraid that I got a good hold of the roots in the first jump and held on for dear life till I could stabilize myself and get a grasp on the edge of the opening. It was too narrow for me to pass through. I hurriedly dug some of the rubble away.

I had to take off my shield and let it fall down the pile. Of course, I was loath to leave it, but that demon could enter any time. Perhaps I could come back for it later. I pulled myself up and emerged into the sunlight in a second. However, I still had to pull myself out of the hole. I was struggling desperately when I saw a woman standing over me, looking down. She was the same one who had been singing; I recognized her blue dress and even in the predicament I was in, I was struck by her beauty. She had deep black eyes, luscious red lips, long black hair and was wearing a strange, shiny blue, tight-fitting dress that covered her from head to toe. She just stood there and didn't bother to help me. I called out to her, 'Fair lady, please help me!'

But instead of stretching out her hand to me, she suddenly bent over right near my face and looked straight into my eyes with an expression full of hate. It shocked me. She hissed at me and I saw she had two long fangs. The next moment, in the flicker of an eye, she disappeared. Instead there was a brightly coloured cobra right next to me, the same one I had seen on the first day. 'Oh no!' I almost screamed, realizing she was a nagin. The serpent opened its dreaded hood, staring at me with its beady eyes, and lunged forward. I quickly covered my face with my arm to save myself and the snake's mouth bit the bracelet on my wrist. Of course, I made that amazingly adroit move intentionally, but its success surprised me as much as it did the snake. It lunged at me again from another angle but I was able to parry its bite again with my bracelet. I knew I couldn't keep this up. I squiggled and squirmed frantically and let myself fall back into the dark hole. Better that demon lurking below than this clear and present deadly nagin. I slid down the rubble. I ignored the pain from the chafing and quickly gathered myself. I hurriedly collected my shield and scrambled down the rest of the debris. I scrabbled desperately to get up and dashed out of the fissure back into the dark cellar. I knew the snake would come after me and maybe that superfast demon too. I was back in the Stygian nightmare. I quickly pulled out one of the magic flares I had brought from Sikkinsala and looked away as I ignited it. At once the chamber lit up, brilliant white. That would deter any serpent or jinn. Throwing the flare behind me, I started running like crazy. The glare lasted for several moments as I negotiated the various items of furniture, my adrenaline giving me speed. And then pitch darkness returned.

Fortunately, I was now near the steps, but because of the effect of the blazing light I couldn't see anything in the blackness, even though now I should have been near enough to spy the slight light from above the steps. Panic-stricken I bumped into one object after another and was worried that in my blindness I could very well lose my bearings and head off in the wrong direction.

However, the next moment I careened into the side wall of the entrance and saw the light from above. I bolted up the steps and closed the slab behind me. It seemed to fit into place with a click. I was safe, I hoped.

I collapsed on the ground, my loins and knees quivering. I was incapable of moving and utterly traumatized. It took me a few moments to gather myself. I soon recovered my breath, seemed to regain control of my limbs, and then I began to feel the pain from my skinned knees and elbows and a myriad other abrasions and scratches. I had slid down over six feet of stone and rubble. My boski shirt was torn and dirty and spotted with blood. I had had an unbelievably narrow escape twice. Boy, I couldn't help feeling that if it came to it I'd rather be roasted to death by a fire demon than suffer paralysing cold. But what I couldn't get over was the utterly venomous nagin. There was something personal in her glare. She hated me. But why me? I hadn't done anything to her. I had never even seen her before. Why, oh why, was I always running into these ravishing, beautiful supernatural creatures bent upon killing me? At any moment the serpent could slither into the library from outside or the demon could burst open the trapdoor. Limping and groaning, I hobbled away from this nightmare place as fast as I could. I painfully mounted my horse and galloped back at full speed, putting miles between me and those malevolent, horrific creatures.

Fortunately, the family were out when I got back; they had gone to Sarmpur for shopping, which was good since they didn't see the condition the servant saw me in when he took my horse. I quickly bathed, washed my cuts as best I could, using cologne as an antiseptic, and changed. Then I waited anxiously for their return. I was still scared that either the demon or the nagin might follow me back, even to this place. After all, what was there to stop them. My brain was filled with wild, fantastic thoughts. In my mind I kept seeing the beautiful face of the changeling serpent and her expression of hate. It was clear she disliked me intensely for some reason. I suspected that she had been observing me since the first day I arrived at the ruins and had seen her in the form of that colourful snake.

Obviously there was something here that I didn't know about, yet it involved me. And following this abstruse logic I arrived at the conclusion that it must somehow concern Koyel. Yes! What else could it be? This meant that she was alive and this nagin knew her, indeed, had some close relationship with her! However, I had more chances of having a civil conversation with a tarantula than her.

Of course, this was only a theory, but I knew I was right, despite all the evidence against it. To me the hate in those beautiful eyes countered any logic to the contrary. I also decided that as is true for any place anywhere, here or in the unknown, the situation couldn't remain static. Things must be happening there and there must be connections between the people or rather creatures there. I hoped Koyel was safe. It seemed hazardous to have a vicious nagin as an enemy. One thing was certain. The demon of air had told me to stop interfering, which meant my search was not going unnoticed. Both the demon and the nagin were determined to kill me. Horrible possibilities gripped me. It seemed awful things were happening out there. I couldn't control my wild imaginings. Then it hit me that events seemed to be moving towards a climax. Something was going to happen out there very soon. Don't ask me for the logic behind this notion, but it came upon me like an obvious corollary. I was on the right track, but how was I to find Koyel or bypass these dreadful creatures.

'Oh Koyel, somehow or the other I will find you,' I uttered to myself, alone in that sunny old house with the lush green orchard outside.

~

'You're home early today; the demon gave you the day off?' Changez remarked when they returned home around three o'clock.

'Did Abdur Rahman give you lunch?' asked Maasiji.

I can't tell you how relieved and happy I was to see them. It was the normalcy of their friendly company after the insanity of that maelstrom full of deathly creatures five miles away that made me feel secure, and immediately my dark and crazy thoughts began to ebb away, although I knew that if by some awful chance one of those dreadful creatures ventured out here my companions would prove scant protection and I'd have to defend them instead.

'I am glad to see you all,' I said, hugging them.

'Hmmm! Cologne, and you're all spruced up and dressed. I tell you, all this about demons is a ruse and Mehran's up to something fishy in the ruins,' Changez said flippantly.

'How'd it go today?' asked Tabrez. 'Did you find the secret chamber?'

'Yes, I found the secret chamber but the demon I was searching for wasn't there. Instead the second demon that Maasiji told me about was there. I escaped by the skin of my teeth.' I didn't tell them about the nagin.

'Are you sure it wasn't just some poor banjara seeking shelter in the ruins?' remarked Changez.

'I wish you could have seen him, he was almost as ugly as you. I assure you it was a demon and a demon of air. He shot out ultra-cold waves that almost froze me, but I got away in time.'

'That does it!' said their mother emphatically. 'You are not going back there tomorrow, under any circumstances. I'm going to phone your mother and tell her to forbid you.'

'Oh please, please, don't do that, Maasiji!' I pleaded.

'Tomorrow is the most important day. You must let me go tomorrow. Just one more day, that's all I need. I promise I won't go there again after tomorrow. Please! I beg of you.'

She must have seen the utter emotional need in my eyes and relented. 'All right, one more day, that's all. But don't do anything dangerous tomorrow. No hunting around secret chambers.'

'By the way, Mehran,' said Tabrez, 'we saw your friend, the halfling you told us about, in the market today. He looked like a normal person.'

'Yes. He drove by in a jeep. Not many people have a car in Sarmpur, that's why we noticed him,' Changez remarked. 'I recognized him immediately as the amil from that night ages ago. He has hardly changed, except he looks well groomed and respectable now. It was definitely him, I told Tabrez.'

~

That night when I went to bed I was filled with restlessness and a sort of fey fatalism. I looked out of the window. There were clouds in the sky and I saw that the moon was almost full. It would be full tomorrow, which is when the portal to the other world would be open. I was so knocked out by the day's events I fell into a deep, dreamless, almost unconscious sleep at once, and so it was surprising that I suddenly woke up in the middle of the night feeling an intense presence in the room. Even as the curtains of sleep slowly lifted from my mind, I realized that this was a familiar feeling. My heart leapt with joy when in the bright moonlight from the window I beheld a shadowy female form that I recognized immediately. For a moment I felt disoriented; I didn't know where I was and thought I was back in Zeenat Mahal.

'Koyel! You've returned,' I cried ecstatically.

'Hush! Yes, Mehran bhai,' she whispered, leaning close to me, and I was back in the dark but luminescent, moon-washed room. 'I can't stay. I have only come to warn you. You must stop searching for me. You don't know who you are up against. If you keep looking for me here, you will get slain. Whatever fate has in store for me I must accept, but I will not be able to bear anything happening to you. Even though we are apart, the thought that you are alive somewhere and enjoying life gives me happiness. You must go away and not risk your life further.'

'I can never be happy without you. Tell me where you are. How can I reach you?'

'No. Don't talk like this. I am not for you. There is nothing I can do, except warn you to go away and not interfere.'

The scene seemed to waver like a mirage.

'Koyel! Wait! Don't go just now. Tell me where you are!'

She became hazier and then she was gone. Only the empty moonlit room remained as though nothing had happened at all. It all seemed so fantastical, as if it was just a dream. I was very upset by what she had told me, but it only made me more determined to find her. If death was the alternative to giving up my search, so be it! I was reminded of a poem by Alfred Noyes that I had read in school:

> Then look for me by moonlight,
> Watch for me by moonlight,
> I'll come to thee by moonlight, though hell should bar the way.

9

Beyond the Horizon

One thing about the desert is that the mornings and evenings are very beautiful. As I shaved the next morning, the sky looked extra colourful and fresh with clouds refracting the golden rays of dawn. I wondered where I'd be come nightfall. I instinctively felt this would be the final day either of my search or of my life. Today this longing in my heart would find some denouement, one way or another. Now I had come to view the air demon as my real foe. He was likely to be my executioner; that was where my danger lay. And knowing that the woman I loved was alive and that Dajaar hadn't killed her lessened my hate for him. He had either spared her life or been unable to kill her, which is what he had been ordered to do. Both eventualities seemed implausible, but here we were. In this situation, it was more important for me to protect myself from the second demon. As for Dajaar, I didn't know how I would tackle him, so I didn't think about it. I would have to play that by ear when, and if, I found him. Thus, I set out. I felt the occasion called for a great quotation, but I could not think of any. I only had one Sikkinsala flare left.

I bade a hearty farewell to Changez and Tabrez and set off for my tryst with destiny. By now the day had turned cold and dreary and the sky was covered with clouds. I searched the ruins for hours. I wandered around, not really knowing what I should do. I had more or less combed the whole area, knocked on all the walls, found the secret chamber, and now I was just pottering around, hoping my weapons would turn shiny again. I began to get discouraged. Maybe there was no tryst with destiny after all. As for my serpentine watcher, either she was doing a good job so I couldn't detect her or she had given up after yesterday's encounter. Anyway, I kept a tight hold on my sword all the time.

Around noon I was walking near where the outer wall had fallen, and lo and behold! I saw footprints on the ground. They had been pressed into the mud and once the sun had dried them, the wind couldn't blow them away. They were rather big. I followed them and they seemed to disappear near a small ditch full of rubble and thorny bushes. There were more of the same footprints in this place. What interest could anyone have in this ditch full of rubble? Something bright red on a bush caught my eye. I examined it and found it to be a scrap of cloth that had got caught on a thorn and torn off. The colour of the cloth was that of the robe I had seen the halfling wearing. Judging from its condition, I concluded that it couldn't have been hanging there for longer than four or five days. This was interesting, because Maasiji had said there was some connection between him and Dajaar. He had been present during the demon's first visit, and when I thought about it I remembered the halfling had also come to Lahore when the demon was scheduled to get me. At that time it was unlikely that he knew I had the missing pendant – yes, I figured that out, or rather Sru cued me in later. It was only when the lamia attacked me that she saw I had it. So this derelict ditch held some important secret for me and I had to find it. There was nothing else I could do but search the rubble.

First I chopped away the bushes, which was easy with my magic sword. Then I began to remove the rubble, which was very difficult because the debris was of large fragments of masonry. Not only was moving them arduous, it was risky as well, since I had to put down my sword and divert my full attention and use all my strength to remove the large masses. Anything could attack me.

Slowly I uncovered a large crevice underneath. I wondered if this was the demon's lair. Was he inside or not? It seemed the opening had been deliberately blocked. Was that to hide the entrance? No doubt a powerful demon could easily move and replace the rubble, but what an inconvenient way to camouflage the cave, and how did he replace it once he was inside? No, there was more to this than met the eye and I suspected that somehow the halfling was involved. It took me almost half an hour to open a portion big enough for me to enter.

I was stunned by the chamber I found inside – a large, round vestibule plunged in darkness, except for the light from the entrance. The chamber had arches all around a central enclosure, and in the darkened galleries on the other side of the arches there were several tunnels leading off in various directions. Apparently in his long sojourn here the demon had dug himself a veritable kingdom underground. The vestibule was encircled by a deep, narrow ditch. At first I thought it must be for drainage but it was too deep and not wet. At the opposite end of the chamber, there were steps leading up to a big door in the facade of rocks and I could spy a line of light under the slit at the bottom. That must be Dajaar's chamber. Sure enough, my weapons were gleaming ready for use. I stepped over the ditch and quickly walked across and mounted the steps. When I reached the door I hitched my shield up on my shoulder and keeping my sword ready in my other hand I reached out and tried the doorknob. I was very tense and my heart was beating. This was the moment of truth.

The door was unlocked. I wondered what I'd find and how whatever ensued would end.

I could never have imagined the scene I witnessed in the chamber.

~

The room was brightly lit by several torches. It was obviously a bedroom, with a marble slab on a dais in front that was clearly a bed, with crumpled bedclothes on it. On one side was a large cage-like brazier, but the coal was not burning and it was very chilly in the chamber. On the bed lay a grotesque figure with goat's legs. This was Dajaar; I immediately recognized his ovine legs and the other scent I had smelt that night. But he looked incredibly old, wizened and wasted. His gargoyle-like face was sunken and pale and his eyes upturned as if he was about to die.

Dajaar looked surprised when I entered. 'Oh! Who are you? Where have you come from?' he moaned. 'You want to check if I'm dead yet.' He lay helpless in his weakness.

Who could have dreamed I'd find this demon in such a weakened condition. Had he reached old age? I thought demons lived for thousands of years. This was a lucky break.

'No, Dajaar, I am not your enemy. I only want to ask you a few questions.'

'Oh please, sir, don't hurt me! Don't hurt me! I have suffered enough. I have been horribly betrayed.'

'No, I have no intention of hurting you,' I assured him.

I told him who I was and the purpose of my visit. 'I want to know what happened on the night of the red moon when you came to kill my cousin.'

'Yes, I remember you well from that night. You were the one who practically carried your mother down the stairs that fateful night because you thought she could be in danger,' he rasped. 'You are a kind person, manusya. Oh please, don't harm me, sir! Please have mercy. I have suffered enough. I am a most unfortunate person who has been treacherously betrayed. I used to be one of the most powerful jinns of agnidesh. But look at me now. I do not have the strength to get out of bed. I have been left here to freeze and starve. No doubt I will be dead in a few days.'

He began wailing and crying. I couldn't possibly question him like this. So I went and began to console him, patting him on the back.

'There! There! Don't cry. I'll help you.' I tried to comfort him, but he cried, even more heartbroken now, and I had to put my arm around the horrible creature.

What the heck! Here I had come all the way to confront the demon who had killed my ancestors and had once come to assassinate my beloved, and instead I was placating and mollycoddling him. 'What happened to you? Who betrayed you?' I asked.

'That treacherous mongrel. That halfling. You know him. You killed his mate. Oh, why did your family give the taweez to him?' he blubbered.

'Nobody gave him the taweez. He stole it. He did this to you?'

'Yes. The vile creature used to be a mere human once, a sorcerer,' he said, gulping, and continued weakly, 'He used his magic to gain the powers of a demon and I helped him in this. You know, not only was I the most powerful demon in agnidesh, but I also knew some magic, which I taught him. In this manner he acquired great power and wealth. But he was not content with this; he wanted to be one of the mightiest demons ever. I didn't suspect anything when suddenly he walked in here about a week ago, and he was wearing that dreadful bauble so I couldn't do anything to him. He used his magic to drain my power and life force and absorb it himself. He ruined me and reduced me to this derelict skeleton that you see and there was nothing I could do. Now I will die soon. Oh, how I regret ever having helped that crafty villain,' he exclaimed.

'And he . . . he has now become the most powerful and dreadful demon of all. Not only are his demonic powers enhanced but so is his magical capability. It's frightening to think of such a powerful being. Nothing can stop him. Who knows what he can, and will, do. He is an invincible monster, I tell you,' the demon hissed vehemently in his debilitated condition.

'Oh, so that's why he wanted the necklace,' I said. 'Anyway, you better answer a few questions of mine, otherwise you'll find out I'm not such a kindly guy,' I said, deciding to get tough.

'Yes! Yes! I'll help you as much as I can,' he stammered.

'Tell me what happened the night of the red moon when you came to kill my cousin Koyel Hashtpuri? What did you do? Did you kill her?' I asked anxiously.

'Please, sir, don't hurt me. Yes, I was sent by the old ones to kill her, but the truth is I didn't.'

So there it was. I knew it. I had been right all along. Of course, those visitations were not delusions. But I couldn't understand what had happened. How could the curse have been averted, and how could the sequencer's intimation and Maasiji's divination about the demon killing his victim have been wrong?

'I heard you killed somebody that night, a young girl?' I asked him.

'Yes, that was a servant girl who was possessed by an evil spirit. That abominable halfling asked me to do this so that the evil spirit inside her could take over the body of the girl completely and she could become his companion. The things I did for him and this is how he has repaid me,' he said ruefully.

'Oh, so that was the poor girl who died that night,' I said, beginning to understand what had happened. Then turning to him again I asked, 'What did you do to my cousin that night? Why did you spare her?'

'I was sent to behead her. I didn't mean to spare her. I had positioned myself next to the nawab so that when she ran up to take the taweez I could slice her head off. But at the last moment somebody threw a cloak of darkness over everything and snatched her away.'

Now this fitted in with what I had seen that night.

'Who did this?'

'I found out later that it was a demon of air. I don't know who he is but I've seen him wandering around here occasionally.'

'Yes, I had a run-in with him too. He tried to kill me, but I managed to escape.'

'Then you are very lucky,' Dajaar commented, 'but he is the only one around here who could have done that on that fateful night. Why he wanted to kill her himself I don't know.'

'You mean he took her because he wanted to kill her?'

'Of course, what other reason could there be.'

'It strikes me that by acting against you in that manner he was taking a big risk. Surely there must be a more cogent reason for him to interfere like this?'

'Don't you think I've thought about this over these years? I, the greatest aseerva Dajaar, was unable to fulfil my assignment. I was too ashamed to return and face the old ones. That's why I took up sanctuary here. But I must say it's a nice place and I liked it, until a week ago.'

The thought of Koyel in the hands of that evil demon gave me the shivers. But somehow she was still alive, I knew that.

'But, Dajaar, she is still alive. I'm certain,' I said passionately.

'What? Impossible! How could she have escaped that devious pariah?'

'She's alive. She came to me twice in a sort of visitation and then disappeared, first time about a month ago, then again last night. I've been searching for her since the first time. I've got to find her.'

A realization crossed his dimmed eyes. 'Oh, so that's why you're looking for her,' he said, patting my hand with his claw. 'Poor boy, you are suffering from some delusion.'

'Who is this aerial demon?' I asked.

Dajaar looked slightly pensive.

'He probably serves some dark lord of a kingdom nearby. After all, he doesn't live here like I do, nor does he go back to agnidesh, yet he keeps coming here occasionally,' he wheezed. He was certainly making an effort to be helpful.

'Dark lord? Kingdom? What do you mean?'

'There is a vast kingdom of snakes here. It extends right up to Thatta. It is ruled by a powerful sheshnag, who is over five hundred years old. It is said he has demons to do his bidding. Probably this demon serves him.'

'Then it is possible this aerial demon might have snatched my cousin for the sheshnag,' I deduced.

'That is impossible. What would such a great king want with a little chit of a girl? No doubt she was a princess in your world, but such things make no difference to the sheshnag. The snakes dislike humans and want nothing to do with them. That is why their mighty kingdom is mainly underground and humans aren't aware of it, though some travellers claim they have seen hordes of snakes performing strange rites on moonlit nights.

'They say that once every hundred years the sheshnag takes a human as his wife in order to propagate his race of nagas and nagins. But your cousin was too young for the sheshnag or any naga to be interested in her. Yes, sometimes the snakes grab children to offer them as sacrifice or to feed them to their wild animals. That's the plain truth,' he said, patting my hand again. I wished he wouldn't do that.

'I feel that the halfling had something to do with this,' I said, voicing my conviction.

'Impossible. If the aerial demon belongs to the sheshnag, he will never obey anybody else.' He had a coughing fit.

'I feel there is one nagin who in fact knows my cousin.

Therefore, she must be in this kingdom of snakes and she must be alive,' I surmised.

'That's impossible. That is an abode of snakes. No outside demons or humans are allowed to go there. If anyone learns about the kingdom, the snakes quickly track them down and kill them before they can tell anyone. Thousands of snakes live there and an outsider would not last five minutes down there. So no matter how you view the situation it leads to the same conclusion. I mean if she's alive, where has she been for twelve years? Why hasn't she returned home, except for your two encounters? I'm sorry to disillusion you, kind manusya,' he said, his voice lapsing into a hoarse whisper again.

'No! No! Everybody tells me that but I keep getting signals that she is alive. In fact, on her last visitation she warned me not to interfere, or I would die; she confessed her feelings for me but gave me to understand that she was betrothed to another. Surely my imagination didn't dream that up.'

'What can I say. You are distraught.'

'Tell me, how do I get to this kingdom?' I asked.

'I'm sorry, I don't know. The entrance is a secret. Nobody other than the snakes, nagas and nagins know. It is well hidden. Neither you nor I will ever be able to find the portal, let alone cross it. And if by some chance we get to the other side, the serpents will immediately kill us.'

Well, it was a cinch I couldn't ask the aerial demon or the nagin. I had met Dajaar and found out what I could. But where could I go from here?

'Please, sir! Please, sir!' the emaciated demon cried, trying to attract my attention.

'Yes, what is it?'

'Please, sir, I've told you all I know. I can see you've got a flask. Can you give me some food please, kind sir?' He could hardly speak.

I gave him the sandwiches Maasiji had prepared for me. He practically grabbed them from my hand and swallowed them in two bites. I wanted to warn him about eating like that after starving for a week.

'And please, sir, can you do me another kindness? Light the fire in the brazier please,' he begged.

I did this for him too; after all, the creature had tried to help as much as he could. But then I saw a spasm wrack his body and he began breathing loudly and hoarsely. Yes, he was dying. Well, he had told me all he could and I had no more use for him, so why should I be bothered. I certainly had no cause to feel sorry for him. Who knows how many of my ancestors he had slain and he would have killed Koyel too had it not been for that off-chance. Still, I remembered a man-eating leopard my father had once shot and everybody had praised him for killing the menace, but I couldn't help feeling sorry for the dead feline because it was only acting according to how nature had created it.

'You're in a bad way. Is there anything I can do to help you?' I asked, much against my better judgement.

'I don't think so. Are you a virgin?'

'Yes, unfortunately.'

He looked a bit surprised, which was a sad comment on my life.

'Then you can help me, kind sire. I need to be given the communion of life from a virgin, preferably female, but I suppose male will do.'

'What is that?'

'Just a little blood. Not much, just a thimble full. Please, kind sire, I've tried to be as helpful to you as I could. I've told you all I know. I will surely die if you don't help me,' he said, looking at me pleadingly.

Nuts! No way! Not on my life. But even that ugly creature's eyes could look beseeching, and his helpless plight melted my heart. I suppose this was the result of playing those namby-pamby games with Koyel as a child.

'Okay,' I said resignedly, taking out my pocket knife. I made a cut on my thumb, which hurt a lot, and then I had to let him suck it, which felt very, very icky. I had heard one feels warm and happy when one does a good deed or an act of mercy, but I assure you I felt nothing of the sort. Afterwards the horrible creature lay back on his bed and he seemed to be more at ease.

'Thank you, kind sir,' he said gratefully.

'Okay. I better get going. I hope you'll recover your strength now.'

'Yes, thanks to you. You've saved my life. Before you go, I must warn you. Beware of the halfling. He has vowed he will take revenge for his mate. If that monster catches you, there will be no escape. He can use his powers or his magic to kill you, which he is determined to do. Get out of here as soon as possible. He has taken up his abode in the old sarai behind the ruins, so avoid that side. However, he has his spies everywhere. Even now he could be coming in this direction, so leave this place as fast as you can,' he said earnestly, holding my hand.

I quickly left the chamber. I certainly didn't want any more of his gratitude.

~

When I stepped out of the room I saw the nagin in the vestibule, with hundreds of snakes around her. They were so many that their musty, hydrogen-like smell assailed my nostrils. As soon as they saw me they reared up, hissing and opening their hoods. Then I realized what I thought was a drain was actually a moat to keep out snakes, but the nagin had put a plank over it near the entrance to enable her companions to cross over. I was trapped. The exit was blocked by the serpents and they would slowly come forward and get me.

As I watched, the nagin took out a been and began to play a haunting melody. All the snakes started dancing. They moved as if there was not a bone in their bodies, in an undulating, sinuous manner that was eerie in its strangeness. I knew that if I tried to dash back to the bedroom, they would dart forward and get me. How many would I be able to slay with my magic sword before the fatal bite! As they danced, they slowly moved towards me in a rippling motion, like the tide breaking on the shore. The scene and the music were hypnotizing and I looked on entranced. It was a beautiful dance of death and despite myself I couldn't help just standing there, enthralled. Once I came to my senses, I did the only thing I could. I took out my last magic flair and averted my gaze to ignite it. Once again there was that blinding flash and everything appeared in unrealistic chiaroscuro momentarily. Immediately the tableau in front of me fell into disarray and I jumped right into the midst of the serpents as that was the only way out. I had to dash towards one of the tunnels since the entrance was too far away. The serpents remained dazzled for a few seconds. Fortunately, I was wearing my riding boots and I stepped on several squishy forms. I leapt over the moat and ran towards the shaft. Seeing the dark, dank entrance, I hesitated for a moment. I saw the nagin had crossed the moat too but instead of coming after me she was moving the plank to enable her companions to follow her. I whipped out my pistol and shot her twice. I couldn't have missed at such close range but the bullet hardly seemed to phase her.

Without another thought I darted into the dark abyss. I found the place was a veritable labyrinth. In the dark I could feel other openings along the walls. At first I simply hurtled along as fast as I could in the blackness, holding out one hand to touch the wall so that I knew which way the tunnel was going. I turned this way and that at every opportunity, trying to complicate my path. I kept bumping into things and tripped again and again but I would hurriedly scramble up and continue my flight. The echoes in the tunnel told me the horrible creatures were hissing and slithering after me. I could visualize the myriad slimy forms gliding along the ground in the tunnels, splitting up into groups and taking different routes. I wouldn't be able to throw them off my track. Then I realized that silence rather than attempted speed would aid me better. I did my best to control my panting, and using my sword as a cane to find my way in the pitch darkness, I moved silently as fast as I could. I had completely lost my bearings by now. Would I be able to find my way out of here? One problem at a time. I stopped to catch my breath, which had more to do with an instinctive reaction of holding it in and fear rather than tiredness. The place was pitch-black. I couldn't see anything. Every sense alert, I listened intently to see if I could hear my pursuers. Often I thought I heard something but there was nothing. There wasn't even any wind down here and the air was stuffy. I wondered if snakes could see in the dark like cats. But this place was so dark even a cat wouldn't be able to make out anything. I couldn't even see my hand in front of my face. All I could see were small spots before my eyes colliding in the dark. For all I knew there might be snakes right next to my foot.

Then I heard them. A low, rustling, scraping hubbub. They were still on my trail. I hoped they wouldn't turn into this tunnel. Then I noticed I could dimly discern the outline of the entrance into this tunnel, and as it appeared to get more definite I realized it was a light in another shaft that was drawing closer. I looked behind me and though it was still dark I saw I was sitting beside a high rock. Without hesitation I clambered on top of it as best I could and looked down. The light behind me seemed to reach right to the entrance of the tunnel, casting dancing shadows and a dim glow into the shaft. In that effulgence I saw a whole stream of slithery black forms gliding like a flowing river on the ground below me. Seeing the set purpose with which they moved as silently as possible in the dim light was a very frightening sight. I thanked my lucky stars that I had climbed on to the rock.

The light became brighter and I saw the nagin was following them holding a lantern. I was just slightly above her head. If I reached out, I could touch her. All she had to do was raise her head and look back. I held my breath and didn't move a muscle. In the close chamber I could smell the snakes. I could even smell the nagin, a mixture of the odour of serpents and a female aroma. In my fear my body began to emit a nervous smell. I had heard that snakes have an acute sense of smell. I hoped that would not give me away. I expected her to look up any moment and spot me. However, she was so intent on her search that she continued moving forward with her lantern. I waited for a long time till the glow of the light had vanished completely. That was a narrow escape if there ever was one. I climbed down and scurried off in the opposite direction, trying to put as much distance between myself and that venomous horde.

It was amazing how quickly I had learned to move in the dark, like a cockroach scuttling along, feeling its way. I was very scared of stray snakes lurking in the dark. They could be anywhere. I hoped my sense of smell would warn me in case I came near one. I could smell the dank fetor of the rocks. Mixed with that odour I got a whiff of a somewhat more organic, alien tinge. It must be a snake! I immediately stood stock-still. Perhaps it would miss me in the dark. Cautiously I ran my hands on the wall of the tunnel behind me. I thought I felt a ledge some distance up. I had no way of knowing how wide it was but I quickly turned around and clambered on top of it, having to swing my legs up because there was no room to pivot my body there. The best I could do was just lie balancing half on, half off on a slight, irregular outcrop of rocks, holding on to the fissures in the wall to prevent myself from rolling down. Then I heard a hiss from below and realized the snake now knew of my presence. I wondered how long I would be able to hang on to this precarious ledge. The hissing became more and more vehement and my heart sank when I realized there were other snakes as well.

I was a goner! I couldn't remain balanced up here for very long and didn't know how many snakes there were below me. Any moment now the snakes below would be joined by the main body of serpents and the nagin with the lantern. Probably the serpents were also handicapped by the dark as much as I was, so my best bet was to jump down, rely on my boots to protect me and swing my sword around as much as possible in the dark. I lowered my legs, put my boots against the little support I could find and jumped. I bumped my knee but managed to more or less make a three-point landing. Quickly wheeling around, I swung my sword again. My trusty blade came to my rescue again and at once blazed up. Now I could see the snakes. They slithered this way and that and lunged at me, but I soon disposed of all of them. Snakes have a creepy trait – even after their head is lopped off, they keep wriggling around. I hoped I hadn't missed any and scurried away from there.

The labyrinth was vast; it was impossible for the serpents to infest all of it. I wondered why Dajaar had made such a complicated network? The thought occurred to me that probably he had used a lot of coal in these twelve years and he had mined it himself here. I could tell there was a plentiful supply of it here. I navigated the tunnels for I don't know how long, but soon I began to feel there were no more serpents, at least not in the section I was in, or perhaps they had given up and gone home. Then I realized the impossibility of finding my way out of this maze. I must have wandered around in the darkness for hours. One fear supplants another. Previously I had been terrified of the snakes finding me; now I was anxious to get out of this trap of claustrophobic darkness. Who knows how complex Dajaar had made these tunnels and if there were any other exits. As I wended my way in the blackness and time kept ticking by, I began to get a feeling of impending doom and started considering the possibility that I might never get out of this horrible place. I was also apprehensive because I wanted to get away from the ruins before dark. I heeded poor Dajaar's warning. I had seen what the halfling had done to that once-fearsome demon. He was no longer the semi-demon who had been scared of Hishoo, and I deduced that so far he hadn't confronted me because he was nervous about my magic sword. Now what Dajaar had told me about him was very frightening, that he had become too powerful to be deterred by such minor things and that, in fact, nothing could stop him. And he had sworn to kill me. He was said to be living in the ruined sarai which was not too far away. Such creatures usually come out at night-time so I wanted to get out before nightfall. I dearly wished I could be home again with my mother and far away from here.

I tried to use my brain. I noticed that in some places the air was stuffier than in others. I decided to go where the air was less stifling because that meant there was more oxygen and such a tunnel might lead to some egress. Sru had thought I was stupid but he underestimated me. When my life depended upon it, I could get my grey cells working. However, it was a pity that even though my life did depend on it I could only find one or two places where the air was better and even these didn't seem to lead anywhere. Finally, as if by a miracle, I saw an exit, an opening and dim light beyond. I was overjoyed; surely my mother's blessings had saved me!

I ran out into the fresh air. The open desert smelt wonderful after the foul smell of the fusty rocks. However, I was disconcerted to find it was late evening already and there were thick, low-lying clouds in the sky that made it seem like it was night; except towards the horizon there was a long clear streak and I could see the last glowing rays of the sun. It was indeed a strange evening with a cloudy night hovering above and only a slit of golden light along the horizon. I remembered an appropriate quotation that I should have thought of in the morning: Chief Crazy Horse on the dawn of the battle of Little Bighorn, 'What a glorious day! What a glorious day to die!' Except this was evening and considering my present situation I didn't like the dying bit. You see, the exit of the labyrinth was outside the outer wall of the old fort and hardly a furlong from the ruined sarai.

~

I quickly started walking back to the broken ramparts. Suddenly I heard a long-drawn-out wail. It seemed to stretch out over the vista of the desert and find harmony in the distance. The voice was female, but not human.

I looked around and saw the nagin walking out from one side of the ruined ramparts and heading towards the sarai. She cried out again in the same manner.

'Shamoon master!' There was reverence and longing in her voice.

With greater urgency she cried, 'Shamoon! Shamoon sire! Come out! He is here.'

Then I realized why she was calling him. How stupid of me to have stopped to see what was happening. The echo of the cry died down and in the fading twilight the incredibly vast expanse of the desert seemed to wait for a moment in silence.

I was going to turn around and run in the other direction when near a clump of palm trees beside the ruins I saw a figure, silhouetted by the dying rays of the sun, walking out. Too late! I thought. Maybe it was better this way: confront the halfling and have it out. After all, powerful or not, he was a coward and didn't have the guts to attack me earlier. Perhaps I could defeat him, after all; otherwise he would always be a sword of Damocles hanging over me, stalking me to take his revenge any time. I took out my sword and stood my ground.

I could tell it was the halfling in his red robe, but he was bigger and more imposing. Something about him filled me with terror. I remembered the awful sensation I had felt when he had passed me on the stairs in Zeenat Mahal. But this was many times more overpowering, even from this distance. There was something infinitely evil and dreadful about him and the purposeful way it was striding towards me. Panic rose inside me. Dajaar was right – he was invincible. He was now close to where the nagin was standing.

'Shamoon, meri jaan, there he is. There he is,' she said, pointing at me.

The halfling answered, 'Thank you, wench. Now I have no more use for you.'

He lifted his hand and brought it down suddenly.

A lightning bolt streaked out of the clouds and struck the nagin. Her scream was cut short and she collapsed to the ground, smoke rising from her form.

'Good heavens! He killed her!' I muttered, awestruck, and quickly turned around to run.

I heard him laugh behind me. 'Ha! Ha! Ha! You can't run from me.'

He lifted his arms and uttered a dreadful imprecation and suddenly there was another flash of lightning and an ear-splitting clap of thunder. A strong gust of wind blew directly against me as I started to run. It came with such force that it almost threw me off my feet. I had to lean forward to take a step as it buffeted me; I could hardly keep my eyes open and struggled to put one pace in front of the other as I tried to run in vain. The fierce gust practically lifted me off my feet and try as I might I just couldn't dash forward. It was like a nightmare in which one was trying to escape from danger but one's steps kept getting slower and slower.

I heard the halfling laugh again. 'That's right. Run. Run as fast as you can,' he taunted and uttered another incantation.

Before I knew it there was a fierce storm blowing across the desert and all around. The wind wailed like a ghost and was accompanied by incessant thunder and lightning. The desert sand blew while the wind kept pushing me back and it was all I could do to prevent being blown towards that malevolent entity striding up.

There was something strange and terrible in the storm. I looked up and to my horror saw that the thick clouds had formed a palpable shape in the sky, like the inside of a tornado swirling upwards. In the dark, inverted maelstrom I could see the full moon riding the black billows. It was a bilious colour, like some travesty of nature.

'Now do you see how powerful I am, you murderous little worm? Now I've got you and I'm going to tear you limb from limb before I kill you,' he shouted above the din of the tempest.

The next moment there was a loud bellow, like a bull roaring.

With difficulty I looked back and saw that Dajaar had emerged from his lair. He seemed to have regained much of his strength.

'I too have some magic I'd like to show you,' he shouted. He was holding a big staff in his hand, which he then struck hard against the ground. At once a huge crack appeared in the earth. It travelled in a zigzag manner at great speed and opened wider. It streaked between the demon sorcerer and me, creating a wide fissure. Dajaar had come to my rescue.

'Now catch him, you treacherous snake in the grass,' Dajaar jeered.

The counter magic had somewhat lessened the force of the opposing wind as well.

'Run, oh human virgin! Get out while you can. He'll soon find some way to cross the crack.'

I didn't need much prompting. I found I could run against the wind now and I dashed off as fast as I could to where I had tied my horse.

I heard that fiend laugh and shout, 'You can't escape me, Mehran Hashtpuri. I'll still get you.'

The storm continued to blow all around. Nature seemed to be raging against me. A fierce wind blew; not a gust like the one that had hindered me, but a swirling cyclonic gale, throwing up whirling dust devils that looked black in the gathering darkness. Soon I reached my horse. It was behaving very skittish. I hoped I would be able to make it stand still enough to mount it.

I was finding it difficult to keep my eyes open in the flying dust. As the storm blew, suddenly some dust devils swirled up around me and seemed to gyrate into several dark, definite masses, sometimes taking the form of humanoids with faces and arms holding metal swords and then turning back into evanescent whirling columns. Without a moment's hesitation, I pulled out my sword. The whirling black figures tried to strike at me as they swished around forming and unforming, but I retaliated, trying to keep all my senses alert. There were three or four of them. They would know how a trained Rajput warrior wields his sword. I countered their blows from one side and then from the other, and when I struck a palpable form it immediately disintegrated into a black spray, but when it was unformed my sword would merely cut through the swirling mass. With many thrusts and parries, sometimes managing to narrowly avoid a stab or a slice, knocking one whirligig aside just in time to turn around and block the lunge of another, and not missing fleeting opportunities to dispose of any of them whenever they arose, I finally managed to get rid of all of them.

I ran to my horse and tried to calm it. But it was very scared and kept kicking and trying to pull out the tether. It was impossible to soothe it and I had to approach it carefully from one side to avoid getting kicked. It took all my doing to untie the tether, and as soon as I was able to loosen it the horse pulled out the cord and started to bolt away. I had kept hold of its rein and made a mad leap to get on top of it. I was unable to settle myself on the saddle and all I could do was to clasp its neck and hang there on one side of the steed for dear life as it galloped off at full speed. I clung on so precariously that its front legs almost kicked my head and I could see the ground underneath rushing by in front of my face, but I was thankful it was going so fast.

The storm continued to rage, accompanied by a dusty wind and thunder and lightning. I was very scared what else it might unleash. With great difficulty I managed to right myself in the saddle and I was just in time. I had hitched my shield on to my back while trying to mount. The next moment I felt a great jolt that almost knocked me off the saddle and there was a brilliant flash all around followed by a deafening clap of thunder. I realized I had been struck by lightning but the magic shield had acted as a lightning rod and saved me and the horse from the shock.

It seemed the storm was bent on attacking me. It whirled all around and several more lightning bolts one after the other hit my shield, jolting me and pushing me about. Other stabs of lightning flashed all around as if aiming for me. I saw one set a small tree on fire. Everything was happening in rapid succession. I had no time to think, only react. The horse galloped for all it was worth and then I saw another one of those swishing dark masses form an indefinite shape in our path. I immediately made my steed jump and the sturdy beast leapt up over the mass like a champion thoroughbred. I could sense the surprise and disappointment of whatever that thing was that was below me. As we landed on the other side I looked back and saw what looked like a tentacle reach out to grab me. I pulled out my sword and struck backwards. The tentacle immediately became a shower of black particles.

As we sped along, I began to feel the storm was no longer centred on me. It had become a regular storm. And then I felt a spattering of rain. I knew I was safe at last. I slowed down and calmed my horse, feeling very grateful towards the beast. I also felt very thankful to the poor demon Dajaar. He had saved me. I hoped with all my heart that the fiend hadn't attacked him in retaliation.

Then I glimpsed a pale form some distance away dash with great speed behind a grove of palm trees. I began to feel uneasy. Maybe I was mistaken about what I saw, or maybe I hadn't escaped all the supranatural creatures abroad that evening.

However, I managed to reach the haveli without further mishap. I breathed a sigh of relief. I could hardly believe I had survived all that had happened and was now safe. As I reined in my horse in front of the gate, there was a desultory flash of lightning and an ominous roll of thunder. It was strange. There were no lights on inside; the place was in darkness and the chowkidar wasn't sitting at the gate.

I dismounted and tethered my horse. I went to the front door and found it was unlocked. The sense of doom I had felt earlier returned or rather I realized it had never really left me.

When I entered the parlour, I felt reassured as I saw Safina maasi and my friends sitting around the fire. Strangely enough they hadn't lit the lamps and the rest of the room was in darkness.

'Hello everyone,' I said. But they didn't respond. Nobody got up. There was no wisecrack from Changez.

'What's the matter? Maasiji, are you all right?' I asked, going up to her, fear rising in my heart. She was sitting on a sofa, and when I put my hand on her shoulder her head lolled down at an abnormal angle; her eyes were open. She was dead.

'Maasiji!' I screamed in sudden grief and shock. In the light of the fire I noticed she had a sharp red line around her neck.

Wildly I turned towards Changez. He was sitting in a chair, and when I touched him he fell down, his head wobbling grotesquely. He too had a red line around his neck.

'No! No! Please no!' I wailed, turning to Tabrez. They were dead. All three of them.

'Thuggees!' I realized and I would have collapsed in grief when something made me look to the back of the room where the dining table was. At first I thought I saw some figures in the dim light in front of the window. There was another flash of lightning outside that momentarily lit up the room. Then I clearly saw three disreputable-looking men wearing turbans standing there.

I was filled with rage. In a reflex action, I whipped out my pistol and shot two of them. Now I was out of bullets. There were others I hadn't seen in the darkened room. At once there was a commotion – cries of rage and some shouted instructions to one another. I felt someone behind me and in an expert motion he slipped a thin cord around my neck, pulled me backwards and jerked me up off my feet with it. It immediately dug so deep it stopped my breath. My tongue was forced out of my mouth, my eyes goggled and I began to feel blackness closing in on me. I could only utter a few guttural sounds as the thin cord hurt and cut deep into my neck. Another snatched the pistol from my hand.

I would have surely died the next moment, but then a voice said, 'Not so quickly. I want him to see who I am.'

It was a familiar voice. A tall figure moved forward, becoming more visible in the firelight. It was the halfling.

The cord on my neck stopped tightening further but remained where it was. I had to wheeze to take incomplete breaths. I was struggling to stay conscious.

The fiend leaned forward, gloating in my face. 'You puny human, who will save you now? I want you to see me before I kill you, you murderous villain,' he said viciously, and one of the thugs lit a candle on the dining table so that there was more light. His physique had changed completely; his whole body, head, height, width, hands and feet had enlarged in an abnormal manner. His eyes had become slits, like a reptile's. There was something repulsive about him and to me he looked more frightening than any demon I'd seen so far.

'Of course, I could easily kill you myself, but this way is better, and these people are very angry at you. You killed their leader,' the unnatural monstrosity continued. 'These people are my followers who practically worship me, have done so for a long time, but now they have found new reverence for me. They have had their eyes on this haveli for several months, and now under my guidance they came to visit your friends. Have you met your friends?'

He laughed victoriously. I still had a trick or two up my sleeve that I'd learnt from grappling with my companions at the polo club. The person behind me was tall and strong and kept me bent backwards so that I could not get out of his grasp or use my hands. But my legs were free. He stood with his feet apart to get a better balance, so I kicked upwards with my riding boots as hard as I could into his crotch. He whooped in pain and the tension of holding me like this made us both fall over backwards. I kicked the dining table as I rolled up to give our fall extra momentum. The motion almost made the cord sever my throat, but he involuntarily slackened the noose as he landed on his back under me and his head hit the floor with a loud crack. He lay there stunned. For a moment I crouched on the floor, coughing and gagging. The person who had my pistol tried to shoot me, but the chambers were empty. Forcing myself to my senses, I whipped out my sword and killed him. The others at once fell back. However, the halfling said, 'Leave him to me.' Turning to me, he added, 'If it's swordplay you want, it's swordplay you'll get.' With a flourish to impress his followers, he pulled out his own Sikkinsala sword from his robes.

We went at each other hammer and tongs. I realized with his new-found powers he would soon defeat me and indeed, he was attacking aggressively and I was only trying to save myself. However, I knew the magical powers of my shield and I let it move whichever way it would to protect me from his onslaught. He kept striding forward and striking this way and that with greater rapidity, but my shield saved me each time. He was getting more and more exasperated.

'I'll teach you a lesson! I'll skewer you like a pig!' he said in his frustration. I kept retreating as he advanced. I deliberately led him to the parlour where the floor was one step lower than the dining room. He was so involved in his onslaught he didn't notice this and almost tripped on the step, but he managed to stabilize himself. Anyway, it showed that ultra-powerful monsters were also fallible.

Then he threw aside his sword. He was feeling bad because he wasn't cutting a good image in front of his followers.

'Forget the swords. I'll fix you up, you tricky little rogue.'

He raised his hand and I knew what was coming. I scuttled away and crouched near the dining table, raising my shield. I expected the fireball, but I had no idea of the magnitude of the one he released. It knocked me back and filled the room with its heat blast. Fortunately, my shield saved me once again. Wow! Any more of those and I would have had it. The dining table caught fire.

The thuggees moved close to their idol so they would be safe. Then he sent a barrage of fireballs, each one like a howitzer shell. They blasted in rapid succession on my shield. One singed my shoulder. He had certainly become very powerful and I knew I wouldn't be able to continue saving myself.

Out of the blue, a thought occurred to me. I remembered wondering why the air demon hadn't cryogenized me near the glass shelf. I felt I had the answer now. The reflection in the glass would send the cold blast back to him. Probably the same principle would work with this monster. I was no match for him, so I tried to use his own power against him. I quickly picked up one of the silver trays of the serving domes lying on the table in the dining room. I tried to hold it in front of my shield so that I'd continue to have its protection as well. The next moment the halfling fired another one of his fireballs, this time the large one again. It knocked me down and flung the tray and shield out of my grasp and burnt my hand. But the incendiary got reflected and went back and hit where the halfling and thuggees were standing. There was a blinding flash and when the fiery blast dissipated, I saw the thuggees lying around, their clothes burning and most of them probably dead. The halfling was tottering around, holding his head, and his robe was smouldering.

This was my chance. While he was still dazed from the blast, I jumped up, pulled out my sword, dived forward and pierced him in the heart. For a moment I stood watching to see him fall. He was taken aback and looked down at his chest. But I was completely disillusioned to see that he didn't fall; instead he looked up at me and laughed. I had totally underestimated him. Even the magic sword couldn't kill him.

'You thought you could defeat me. Me! The most powerful creature there is. Now you don't have your shield, so *die*, you miserable butcher,' he said and raised his hand. This time I had no protection.

As I looked at him, I saw an eerie, porcelain-white face emerge behind him. The next moment there was a freezing blast of air and suddenly I saw the halfling become stationary in the pose he was in, his gloating expression frozen on his face; the next instant he shrank down to half his size, seeming to gleam like glass or ice, and then he shattered into a million pieces. Unbelievably, I had been saved again. It was the aerial demon who had tried to kill me yesterday, so I was uncertain about what he'd do to me. Was I next? Suddenly I felt a sharp pain in my back. Oh no! I had forgotten about the thuggee who had tried to strangle me. He had stabbed me! My whole body went limp and everything turned black.

10

The Kingdom of Snakes

I suddenly found myself conscious, feeling sick, stiff and thirsty. I can't tell you how awful it felt. I coughed and gagged, kept trying to vomit but there was nothing inside me to bring out. Dying would have been better – okay, remaining unconscious would have been better. But slowly I managed to gather my senses. I blinked and looked around and saw I was lying on a comfortable bed in a strange chamber. It was large and seemed to be dug underground, like a burrow, as the walls were obviously earth compacted to smoothness. There was what seemed to be an artificially contrived pool of water on the ground near the bed. The roof was high with well-crafted woodwork and the magnificent drapery gave the room a regal appearance. However, though it seemed to be underground, there was a fresh breeze blowing and even bright sunlight streaming on to one wall, which I noted was coming from a neat system of adjustable funnels attached to the ceiling. There was an odour about the place – a bit rubbery, somewhat like hydrogen gas – that I associated with snakes. This was unbelievable. I was wondering where I was and what had happened when, lo and behold, Sru, that rascally dhakana, walked in.

'Sru! Where did you come from? Where am I?'

'Greetings, Mehran manusya. I'm glad to see you've regained consciousness. You've been out four days. How are you feeling?'

'When I'm capable of feeling anything, I'll let you know,' I answered miserably. 'Where am I? How'd I get here? And where have you turned up from?' I asked in one breath.

'Hush. Don't strain yourself,' the sprite said, comforting me. 'You're all right now. You are in the royal hakeemkhana of the devanagri of Azirakaan. I'm here because the sheshnag often calls dhakanas to work for him. There was to be a big wedding here and we dhakanas were called to cook and serve. I also came along. I half suspected I'd find you here. You know, this is a great kingdom and it's built mainly by us dhakanas. You see these funnels? They were designed by one of my ancestors. They actually bring the sun's rays down two hundred feet to–'

'Sru, tell me what happened. How did I get here?'

'You were attacked by your halfling friend and some murderous followers of his. Somebody stabbed you in the back. He almost killed you. The sheshnag's demon Naagseth saved you and brought you here where the royal hakeems have treated you. You've been in a bad way. Honestly, in the beginning I thought you wouldn't make it. But the royal hakeems are good; they take their knowledge from the old sones of Sikkinsala. They fixed you up.'

I realized that Naagseth must be the aerial demon. 'The demon of air!? He once tried to kill me. I thought he was hostile.'

'Well, he saved you and took a big risk to do so. That halfling had become immensely powerful, much more powerful than Naagseth and could have crushed him like a fly. However, when you killed those thuggees and the halfling was concentrating on you, Naagseth sneaked in and blasted that phoney fiend. They're crafty, these aerial demons.'

Slowly I recollected what had happened and I remembered Safina maasi and my friends.

'What's the matter? Are you feeling sick?'

'No! No! Worse than sickness,' I replied bitterly, wiping my eyes with the sheet.

'Oh, I understand. They were your friends,' he said, commiserating. 'At least you survived. If it's any solace to you, you got their revenge, manusya.'

'Sru, this place where I am must be the kingdom of

snakes?' I exclaimed, suddenly realizing what this meant.

'That's right.'

'Sru! Oh Sru! Can you tell me if you know of a human girl called Koyel living here, or maybe she goes by some other name here?' I asked anxiously.

'Certainly. She's a princess over here. It was her wedding we came to arrange.'

'Oh!' I said, feeling immense disappointment. She had told me she was betrothed to another. I was too late. I almost wished I hadn't survived. What was the point of all I had done now? What was the point of anything?

'Sru, my small friend, you remember that quest I told you about. Well, it was to find this girl,' I told him tragically.

'Oh yes! I guessed all that. Don't worry. If it makes you feel better, I better tell you the wedding was cancelled.'

'Cancelled!' I exclaimed, my heart leaping up inside me.

'Yes, her fiancé called off the wedding and that changed everything. It was quite tragic. He was a naga who was a prince here and the governor of a province. He saw this lady Koyel at a function and liked her. He took a proposal to the sheshnag, who was favourably inclined towards the match. However, when he told the princess about it, she flatly refused to marry the naga. All this happened quite recently, just two weeks ago. The sheshnag made inquiries and found out that the princess was nursing a flame for you. He was very angry.

The nagin who attacked you is this naga's sister. She looked at you as a rival to her brother and a slight upon the family. That's why she hated you. Then that foolish woman met the halfling and she fell in love with him. After that you arrived in the ruins and began searching there. You were getting too close and the naga didn't like it. He complained to the sheshnag. The nagin was spying on you for the halfling, but she wanted to kill you herself,' Sru explained.

'How do you know all this?' I asked him.

'People talk. Probably the servants in the royal kitchen know more about what's going on in the realm than the viziers. When the sheshnag got reports of your activities, he was furious. He told the princess he would have you killed if you didn't go away and reminded her that she was betrothed to the naga governor and would have to marry him no matter what. The naga took this as permission for him to send the air demon to kill you. Yes, I heard about your narrow escape and apparently so did the princess, which is why she was anxious about you and appeared to you that night. Then the next day, you and that aerial demon destroyed the halfling.'

'That's what puzzles me. One day the aerial demon is trying to kill me and the next he risks his neck to save me.'

'Yes, that was strange. What I figure is that earlier the naga had ordered him to kill you, so he was carrying out instructions. However, sometimes such demons develop a sense of loyalty. He often served the princess. When he took her to visit you he found out that she loved you, so then he did his best to save you.'

'Oh, so that's it,' I said. Another thought occurred to me, and I added, 'What about the demon Dajaar? Do you know if he is all right, Sru?'

'Yes, I heard about him. Apparently he went back to agnidesh. Yes, he's all right,' he informed me.

'You told me Koyel was going to be married, but the marriage got called off. What happened?'

'It was cancelled because of the death of the naga's sister. Well, all the inhabitants here were grieved and disappointed about what happened, but as for me' – he shrugged – 'I never liked her and I knew you would be upset about the marriage, so what shouldn't have been came not to be. As you know, the monster killed the naga's sister. The poor naga was so upset by this and disillusioned by the whole affair that he called off the wedding. That changed everything.'

'The wedding has been called off permanently?' I asked timorously.

'So it would seem.'

'Sru, do you think it will be possible for me to see the princess somehow? It's very important for me.'

'Manusya, when I said that the naga called off the wedding and that changed everything, I meant "everything". Overnight from an unwanted intruder you became a hero who faced the halfling and was responsible for helping Naagseth destroy him. Even the naga governor praised you.'

Then he looked at me and smiled. He told me, 'The lady you seek is here and she is waiting for you. But first you have to meet someone else. She has been waiting for you to regain consciousness. I'll just check to see if she has arrived outside. When you see her, you will understand everything.'

'Who is it? Is it Koyel?'

'Well, not exactly.'

'What do you mean "not exactly"?' I demanded.

But he dashed out of the door and came back a moment later with an elderly lady. She was very graceful. I found something ineffably attractive about her. I looked at her eyes and realized they resembled Koyel's.

'This is Her Majesty, the Devanjana of Azirakaan,' Sru introduced her.

She smiled at me. I apologized for not being able to get up.

'It doesn't matter, nephew. You are my nephew, you know. As you might have guessed, I am Koyel's mother.'

~

Some attendants brought in a chair for her. She sat down beside me.

'We were very worried about you. Thank goodness you have recovered,' she told me, her gentle eyes looking at me. 'Yes, you can meet my daughter as soon as the hakeems have examined you and confirm that you are well enough to get up.

'I better explain everything to you,' she continued. 'I was betrayed and cast aside by your family years ago, except by your uncle, of course. At least he tried to stand by me. Your grandfather locked me up in the chamber of snakes, hoping I would get bitten by a serpent and die.'

She sounded quite bitter.

'But as the old adage goes, when one door closes upon you Providence opens other ones. It turned out that the sheshnag who rules this kingdom had seen me previously and fallen in love with me. The old pavilion full of snakes is actually the portal to his realm. So I didn't die that night. The devanagri sent some nagins to me and they brought me to Azirakaan. We were married in a royal and grand style and I became the queen of this kingdom. I could never return to my old world, but the truth is I have no desire to. I have been happy here and have borne the devanagri several nagas and nagins. During that time, I missed my daughter. Then one day I learnt about the curse and realized she was going to die. I appealed to my husband to save her. So he sent Naagseth to rescue her, who brought her here. The devanagri has been very kind and treats her like his own daughter. We have lived here together for years and she grew up among these creatures. However, she never forgot you. She has always loved you.'

'Oh Khala,' I said, overcome by emotion. 'I too have missed her very much.'

She patted my hand. 'I know, I know. The fondness for a companion in childhood can often be the genesis of true love,' she said understandingly. 'Well, let me continue and tell you all that happened. About a month ago she learnt that your life was threatened by the curse. She was frantic to save you. She begged my husband to let her go and warn you. The devanagri sent her with Naagseth to Zeenat Mahal.

'Shortly after that my daughter got betrothed to another naga prince. Frankly, I thought it was a good match. In fact, initially I was against you having anything to do with my daughter because of the way your family had treated me. However, later I got a report of your quest in Sikkinsala. Then I changed my mind because I knew that only a human whose love is sincere can find the portal to Sikkinsala. I realized why my daughter had missed you over these years. You have a right to know all this,' she stated emphatically. 'You must have heard about the tragic circumstances that led to the cancellation of the wedding. You saw that fiend kill the poor sister of the naga.'

'Yes, I saw that.' I wasn't too moved by the death of that venomous and literal femme fatale.

'Subsequently, you confronted that monster and slew him. You showed great courage and heroism. Everybody admires you.'

'Well, it was your demon that slew him. As for me, I'm lucky to be here in one piece.'

'You both did your bit, but you showed immense courage and had to confront him. And I know why you did all this,' she said, patting my hand. 'I was watching everything through the star Zohra. You can't imagine how anxious I was about you when that monster called down that tempest.' She looked pensive for a moment, then with a sphinx-like smile, leaning forward towards me, she told me, 'I also tried to help in my own little way. I've learnt a little magic over the years. When I saw how fierce the storm was, I sent over a rain cloud to dilute the evil magic.

'Well, now you know how I feel about you and my husband is of the same mind. I know what you want,' she said.

'More than anything in the world,' I added.

'Well, there is an important formality to be completed. Since your mother can't come over, this is something you will have to do yourself,' she said, sitting back in the chair.

I guessed that something important was expected of me and for a moment I was nonplussed. Fortunately, Sru was standing by me on the other side of the bed.

'You're supposed to make your proposal,' he whispered.

I will spare you the embarrassing details of my proposal; suffice to say I did it without hesitation. I felt all this was some wonderful dream come true and

I didn't want anything to distract its course. My future mother-in-law became quite emotional and got up and kissed me.

Several questions occurred to me now.

'Err . . . Khalaji, does this mean Koyel and I can never return to my own world?'

'The devanagri and I have considered every aspect of the situation. You will be happy to know the old ones have said you can live in your world. They stated that since both of you are completely human, it will be better if you stay in your own world, but you can come and visit us when you feel like it. However, there is one condition and you must take that very, very seriously – you will have to keep the existence of this kingdom absolutely secret. You mustn't even tell your children. As you know, the old ones have methods to ensure that people keep their secrets.'

'Err . . . there's one other problem,' I ventured. 'The thuggees murdered my dear friends. There's bound to be an investigation about that. In fact, the police are probably looking for me already.'

'Don't worry. You see, though we keep ourselves separate from humans, we are well aware of all your customs and procedures. After killing the thuggees, Naagseth burned down the house completely. The thuggees had killed everybody in that house, even the servants, so apart from you no human knows what happened there. He put your pistol in the hand of one of your friends, so that if there is an autopsy it will seem he killed the two thuggees. That tragedy will remain an unsolved mystery in police records. So you don't have to worry on that score. Your visa is still valid and you have the key to your room in the rest house, so you can go and pay off your dues there and return to your country without arousing any suspicion. When the time comes, Naagseth will come and transport you back here for your wedding. Then Koyel and you can go to Zeenat Mahal. Borders are of no concern for Naagseth. I'm sure you will be able to think up any number of excuses about finding your long-lost cousin after all these years once you are back in Pakistan.'

I was overjoyed that the dream continued getting better and better.

~

I was told Koyel was waiting for me in the garden chamber of the palace. Sru showed me the way. I could hardly contain myself. I swear I never felt as nervous confronting the horrible monsters as I did now.

Sru decided to give me a paternal lecture on the way.

'Since I'm older than you – I'm about two hundred and fifty years, give or take a few decades – and you are twenty-two, I better give you some advice. Don't be disillusioned. It's been such a long time; she was only a child then, so much has changed. You will not be the same people you were when you parted. Though you feel great love for her and vice versa, I believe you will be like strangers meeting again.'

This reminded me of an old verse I had read.

My thoughts and feelings were going haywire as I entered the garden. After all these years and my impossibly long search, I couldn't believe I was finally going to meet Koyel in flesh and blood. But there in front of me she sat. Yes! I remembered the verse:

اب نہ وُہ ہم ہیں' نہ توُ ہے نہ وُہ معاضی ہے فراز
جیُسے دو شخس تمنا کے سرابوں مِیں ملیں -

(Now I'm not him, nor you, you. Even the past is not the same, Faraz
Like two strangers we may meet again in longing dreams.)

But this was no dream.

She got up.

I stepped forward.

'Koyel,' I said, touching her, almost in disbelief.

'Meeru,' she said, and she was about to cry.

And so was I. We looked at each other and fell into each other's eyes and arms and hugged with all our heart and soul. An image flashed in my memory of a lovely little girl and a sweet-looking boy sitting together playing with dolls, and all the years of the joy of being together that we'd been deprived of after that. But at last, in each other's arms, that one moment compensated for all our years of sadness and struggle. Strangers or not, soon we would be completely united. No, this was no dream; it was much more than a dream and one from which I would never wake up.

The rest of my story with my beloved wife is none of your business.

A Note on the Author

Imran Kureshi lives in Pakistan. He is a former employee of the Pakistan State Oil Company Limited and has been a freelance editor of books and PhD theses for over sixteen years. His collection of short stories set in rural Punjab, titled *Billa Nayee and Other Tales*, has been published by Oxford University Press. This is his first novel.

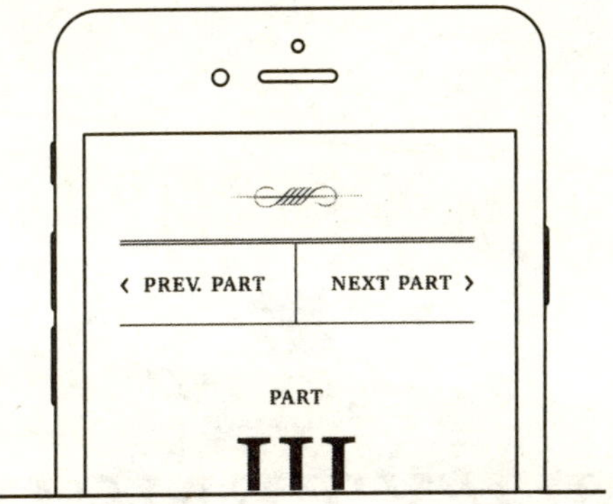

Beautiful Typography

The quality of print transferred to your mobile. Forget ugly PDFs.

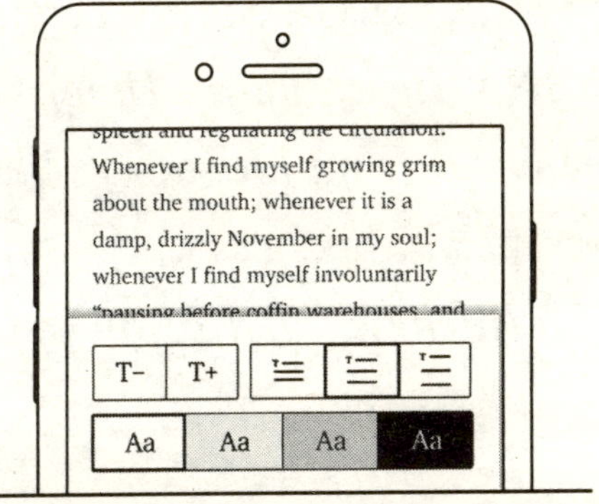

Customizable Reading

Read in the font size, spacing and background of your liking.

AN EXTENSIVE LIBRARY

Including fresh, new, original Juggernaut books from the likes of Sunny Leone, Praveen Swami, Husain Haqqani, Umera Ahmed, Rujuta Diwekar and lots more. Plus, books from partner publishers and loads of free classics. Whichever genre you like, there's a book waiting for you.

CRUCIBLES OF SIN
HITESHA
Can a Geek ever find Love?
Finding Juliet
Toffee
Mary Shelley
Frankenstein
A FAROOQ RESHI INVESTIGATION
COLD FLAKE
PRAVEEN SWAMI
How to Heal Your Broken Heart
A Psychiatrist's Guide To Heartbreak
DR SHYAM BHAT
MOIN and THE MONSTER
ANUSHKA RAVISHANKAR
Mafia Queens of Mumbai
stories of women from the ganglands
S. Hussain Zaidi
with Jane Borges
Foreword by Vishal Bhardwaj
Pakistan's Queen of Romance
UMERA AHMED
Nowhere Girl
A Story of Love & Forgiveness
THE BEHEADING
This Is How He Will Bless Her
ABHEEK BARUA
THE Peshwa
The Lion and the Stallion
THE INVISIBLE WOMAN
SAURBH KATYAL
ANGRY BIRDS FAN? READ THE BOOK!
ANGRY BIRDS TOONS
TOONS TALES
ARCHANA SABOO
ADIKOOL
in
#AfricanAdventures
i am not a bimbette
Tarana Khan
She hates me. He loves me not but...
DON'T FALL IN LOVE
Vandana Shankar
KHUSHWANT SINGH
WE INDIANS

DON'T JUST READ; INTERACT

We're changing the reading experience from passive to active.

Ask authors questions

Get all your answers from the horse's mouth. Juggernaut authors actually reply to every question they can.

Rate and review

Let everyone know of your favourite reads or critique the finer points of a book – you will be heard in a community of like-minded readers.

Gift books to friends

For a book-lover, there's no nicer gift than a book personally picked. You can even do it anonymously if you like.

Enjoy new book formats

Discover serials released in parts over time, picture books including comics, and story-bundles at discounted rates. And coming soon, audiobooks.

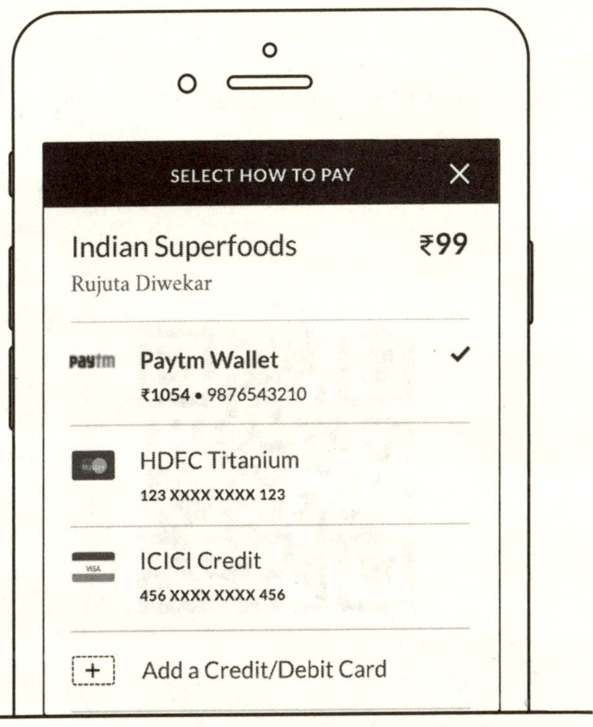

Paytm Wallet, Cards & Apple Payments

On Android, just add a Paytm Wallet once and buy any book with one tap. On iOS, pay with one tap with your iTunes-linked debit/credit card.

Click the QR Code with a QR scanner app
or type the link into the Internet browser
on your phone to download the app.